WHEN WE FELL

AN EXTRA SERIES PREQUEL NOVELLA

MEGAN WALKER & JANCI PATTERSON

For Drew
who stayed

ONE

Blake
Eight Years Before

The first time I meet Kim Watterson, I'm sitting in a rowboat on a little beach in southern Texas, going over the day's script, trying to make sure I have my lines memorized right. My character, Tyler, is about to have his first kiss with his love interest, Alice Stone, right here in this rowboat. Tyler is a chill kind of guy, so I can't imagine he's nervous.

But I sure as hell am.

"Need anything, Blake?" one of the PAs calls to me, and I shake my head and give them a thumbs-up, which makes me feel like I'm about five.

In real-life years, I'm twenty-two, but in Hollywood years, I'm only nine months. My first film just debuted a couple weeks ago, in which I played a side character—the smart-ass friend of the main character in a teen romantic comedy. My agent parlayed that role into another bit part, but given my overall lack of experience, I'm pretty sure it was my looks alone that got me this, my third job—a lead in a beachside rom-com starring opposite Kim Watterson.

My agent was excited to land me such a big role before my

first film even debuted. I was excited to land the part, of course, but even more excited that I'd be acting opposite my teenage celebrity crush, a woman I watched in her teen sitcom, *Spy High*, for most of my adolescent years.

It's only now, sitting here in this row boat and staring at the script, that I'm remembering this means Kim has many, many more years of experience than I have. As she's tried to outrun her child star status, she's done movies with nude scenes, while I've never filmed an on-screen kiss.

I may be about to make a complete fool out of myself, but it's not going to be because I don't know my lines.

"Hey," a female voice says from behind me. "You must be Blake."

I glance over my shoulder and, oh my god, there she is. The great Kim Watterson. She's wearing a tank top and denim shorts, and her long, blond hair falls in waves over her tanned shoulders.

Holy shit, she's even more gorgeous in person. I'm grateful we're shooting this in fall and not summer, because just seeing her in person is making my palms sweat.

Kim is carrying a coffee mug in one hand and a water bottle in the other, which seems like a lot to drink right before a scene, but what the hell do I know?

"That's me. And you're Kim."

"I am." Kim tucks her mug under her arm and holds out her hand like we're in some kind of business meeting. I shake it awkwardly.

When I let go, she reaches into her coffee mug and pulls out a handful of M&Ms, which is unexpected. She pops one in her mouth and then extends the mug to me. "Want some?"

I'm a little stunned by the sight of movie-star Kim Watterson offering me M&Ms out of a coffee mug, but I nod and grab a few. "Peanut and regular M&Ms?" I manage to ask. "Mixed together?"

Kim climbs into the boat, sitting down on the bench at the

6

other end. "It's the *perfect* mix. Two-thirds regular to one-thirds peanut. I always have this mix on the first day of filming. It's good luck." She smiles at me, which makes my heart skip erratically. "Also, it gives me nice, chocolaty breath, which is never bad for a kissing scene."

Being reminded that I'm about to lock lips with this woman doesn't do anything to help my anxiety. I pause for a beat too long, scrambling to think of something to say, which is normally not difficult for me.

I suppose, though, I do have a pretty strong opinion on M&Ms, so I lean into that.

"It can't be the perfect mix without peanut butter," I say.

She wrinkles her nose. Apparently peanut butter M&Ms are out, even though they're clearly the best. "In your extensive experience with perfect candy mixes."

Despite my nerves, I smile. "Because I have a sense of taste, Watterson," I say. "You should try it."

Kim's eyebrow raises, and I die a little inside. I'd meant that to be teasing banter, but I probably sounded like a total dick, and—

Her lips tug up at the sides. "I'll never dilute my perfect mix by adding a lesser M&M," she says primly.

"Not one for trying new things, then."

Her blue eyes flash, and now I definitely think I've crossed the line. Shit.

"Just an observation," I add quickly.

She eyes me for a moment, then shrugs. "I try new things. I just know not to mess with perfection."

Now I'm wondering how terrible an idea it would be to get a package of peanut butter M&Ms and pop them into her mix one at a time. Not very professional, but it might be worth it, just to see how she'd react. "We'll see about that," I say.

Kim gives me a sharp look, and I pop the M&Ms in my mouth and try to look innocent. I also try not to pay too close attention to her lips as she chews. I always thought Kim's character on *Spy High* was beautiful, but in person (and several years older), she's supermodel gorgeous. I've never had a difficult time with women, but she's completely out of my league.

And very soon, I'm supposed to kiss her and make it look natural. I wish Tyler was less confident—I'm not sure where I'm going to drum up the moxie I need for this scene. It doesn't help that I'm not really an actor. A friend of a friend that I met at a surfing competition told me I had "the Hollywood look." Turned out she worked in casting, and she asked me to come to an audition. I thought that sounded hilarious, so I went, and somehow the rest of the casting team thought I was perfect for the part. I landed my first role, got some help finding an agent, then showed up and spoke my assigned lines like a human being. This seems to have been all that's required for my—as my agent puts it—"rapid ascent to stardom."

One of these days I'm going to hit the ceiling of what's possible for a guy just showing up and doing what comes naturally, and I'm afraid today might be that day.

I probably should have quit while I was ahead. The reviews of my (small) performance in my first movie are good, but I very much doubt that will last.

Kim indicates the script in my hand. "Am I distracting you? Not that there are many lines in this scene, but you better know them by the time we start."

"I think I've got it," I say. "They made a couple changes from the copy I had, though. I'm dyslexic. It's hard when they switch things up on me."

This is probably a ridiculously unprofessional thing to say. I know actors have to be flexible, and lines changing up to the day of the shoot—and even during—is part of the job.

She actually looks impressed. "I'm sure they'd get someone to read you your lines, if that would be easier."

"I can read." I probably sound defensive, and maybe I am a little. "It just takes me longer than other people." I take a deep breath. Might as well get that out of the way. "I'm more worried about the rest of the scene. I've never done one of these before."

She smirks at me. "Yeah, I figured. This is your third movie, right?"

"Right," I say. She's apparently done her research.

"I saw your first one. You're good."

I blink at her. "Thanks." I'm not sure what I did that could be defined as "good," but this seems to be the general consensus, and I'll take it.

"So, doing your first kiss scene and first sex scene in the same movie. That would be intimidating."

My cheeks flush. She's not wrong. There's exactly one sex scene in this film, and I'm even more nervous about *that*. I'm glad they didn't pick that scene for our first day on set, and I kind of wish they'd put off the kissing a little longer, too. Let us get comfortable with each other first.

Though I guess we have a few minutes here to accomplish that. "Would you want to rehearse this scene with me? Just to get the jitters out of the way?"

Kim is looking at me like I'm crazy, and my flush deepens.

That was clearly the wrong thing to say.

"Um, no," she says. "I'll read the lines with you if you want, but I'm not going to *rehearse* the whole scene with you."

I should probably play it off like I didn't mean we should rehearse the kiss, but I definitely did. "Yeah, okay. No problem."

"And you should know I have a policy against sleeping with co-stars, and I don't ever break it. So this"—she waves back and forth between us—"isn't happening."

"Okay," I say weakly. "Noted." I didn't have any illusions that Kim Watterson was going to sleep with me. That's definitely not what I meant, but it doesn't feel good to hear it outright like that. "I wasn't hitting on you, though. Sorry if it sounded that way. I just thought we could run the scene to get the nerves out of the way—"

"You're new," she says. "So maybe you don't know, but actors don't just sit around and rehearse kissing scenes. You never know exactly what the director is going to have you do, so what would be the point?"

"Right." My face is still burning. I knew I was going to make a fool out of myself, but I didn't expect it to happen this fast. "Thanks for the tip. I appreciate it."

She stares at me like she doesn't quite believe me.

I sigh. "I'm really sorry. I didn't mean to make you uncomfortable."

"I'm not. As long as you understand that I'm not going to sleep with you."

"I got that." I'm starting to sound annoyed now, which is probably unfair, but damn it, does she have to keep *saying* that?

Kim is a professional. Everyone else in this industry has been treating me like I'm some new up-and-coming actor, but I can already tell that she can see right through me.

Yeah, I definitely should have quit while I was ahead. Now I'm here and under contract, and I'm being paid more money than I've ever made in a year, just to say my lines and be Tyler. (Though I'm told by my agent I'm not making nearly as much money as Kim is for this movie, which doesn't surprise me.)

"All right!" the director, Derek Green, calls from over by the cameras. "Kim! Blake! We're ready for you!" Derek's a beefy guy with a cragged face and a take-no-shit gaze that makes him look like he spent most of his life as a prison guard—not the type of guy you'd imagine directing rom-coms, but apparently he's known for it.

Makeup and wardrobe descend on the boat, taking away my script and Kim's M&M mug and water bottle and doing one last pass over our hair and clothing. Derek gives us instructions, and we sit next to each other in the rowboat still beached on the shore. We're just sitting, not rowing, which is good, because I doubt it's seaworthy. Production buzzes around us. I'm pretty sure I'm the *most* nervous person here, but there seems to be a frenetic energy buzzing around. I've never been present for the first shot of a film before, so I don't know if this is normal.

When everyone is ready, the AD calls "action," and Kim smiles up at me and says her first lines. Her whole demeanor changes as she becomes Alice.

I bet Alice wouldn't turn Tyler down if he asked her to rehearse a kissing scene. Coming from Tyler, though, that would definitely be a come-on. It's surprisingly easy to slip him on like a skin and flirt with Kim—much easier than it would be to flirt with the real Kim, who is even more intimidating now that I've met her.

We stare into each other's eyes, and as directed, I look down at her mouth for a count of ten. They'll cut this down when they edit the film together, of course, but I'm supposed to make sure they have time to get the establishing shots they need.

Then I bend down and kiss her.

I imagined this going terribly every time I read through it. I've kissed plenty of women, but I worried that when it was time to do it for the cameras, I would choke.

Instead our mouths meet like they're meant for each other. Kim tastes like chocolate and lip gloss and something sweet and intoxicating and indefinable. I run a hand through her hair, and she rests hers on my shoulder, and it feels like the most natural thing in the world. Not at all awkward like I thought it would be.

Kim breaks the kiss and bites her lip and smiles. This time it's her turn to count to ten before she kisses me again, with more hunger this time, and I have to fight to remember the cameras are there, that this isn't real, and it isn't going to be. I don't put my tongue in her mouth. I'm pretty sure I'm not supposed to put my tongue in her mouth, but god, I want to.

You should know I have a policy against sleeping with co-stars, she said. *This isn't happening.*

Which means that, with the exception of the sex scene we're filming, this is as close to Kim Watterson as I am ever going to get.

TWO

Kim

I t's late at night at the end of the first week of filming, and I should be asleep already, given how early I need to be up for hair and makeup for tomorrow's shoot, but I'm not. Instead, I'm sitting out on the steps of my trailer in my yoga pants and a comfy hoodie, talking with Blake, who is sitting right across from me on the steps of his trailer, in his own post-work comfort clothes—a pair of loose basketball shorts and a plain t-shirt. We've been doing this the last couple evenings, for longer and longer stretches. At this rate, by next week we'll be getting no sleep at all.

I should be responsible and call it a night and go inside—that's who I am, after all. Responsible Kim Watterson. But I really don't want to. I also don't want to think about what that means.

Or maybe I should. After the awkwardness that first day when I insisted (way more times than was necessary) that I'll never sleep with him, Blake and I have managed an easy on-set rapport. As I've allowed myself to talk to him more between takes and late into the evening, I think he's becoming a good friend.

That's all. Someone who's easy to talk to and fun to be around, which isn't always something I can find on a film set. It has nothing to do with how my heart beats faster when he's around or that incredible kiss we filmed the first day—so different from any of the many, many on-screen kisses I've shared with co-stars.

Nope, nothing to do with *that*.

I sigh. I wish I was dumb enough to be in that level of denial.

Blake pauses mid-story about a friend who stupidly tried to compete in a surfing competition while wasted. He cringes. "I'm sorry. This is, like, the third surfing story I've told tonight, isn't it? I've become one of those people. I will officially shut up now."

It takes me a second to connect him stopping what was a hilarious story with the sigh I just made.

"No, it's—" I'm not going to admit what it really is, which is not me getting sick of his surfing stories. I actually love hearing them. When he first told me that was one of his favorite things to do, I could totally see it—not because he's anything like the stereotypical "nah, bruh" surfer dude, but because there's something about him that makes me think of sunlight sparkling on the ocean. Of cresting waves and bright sky.

Plus, I can only imagine how hot he looks doing it. His auburn hair all wet, the glistening of water on his bare chest . . .

No need to think about that, Kim. Which doesn't mean I won't.

I raise an eyebrow at him. "Is this 'friend' actually you? I need to prepare myself for how much mocking I'm about to do."

He looks offended, but I can tell from him trying to hide a smile that he isn't. Even though it's late at night, I can still see him fairly well—they keep lots of lights on around set at night, for safety and security reasons.

I have to admit, I wish I could see him better. Especially those shifting blue-green eyes of his that I have to stop myself from staring into for too long.

"No, it is not," he says, "because I am not a complete idiot with a death wish, thank you very much. Also, you need to *prepare* for your mocking? Like, are you going to start making lists of insults?"

I shrug. "Maybe. It would be a lot of mocking, and I wouldn't want to forget anything."

He grins, and my heart skips a beat. That smile should come with a warning. "This seems like a very Kim thing to do."

With someone else, I might have been embarrassed, because the truth is, making lists *is* a very Kim thing to do, and I know it's kind of weird. But the way he says it is fond, and I like that even though he's barely known me for a week now—and I spent the first few days trying to keep a very professional distance—he gets me.

"Yeah, well. I'm a very Kim person," I say.

"Don't I know it."

There's a moment where our eyes meet across the short distance between our trailers and hold there. Then he looks away, and there's a little tug in my chest that I do my very best to ignore.

"So are you going to finish the story?" I ask. "Because I'm curious as to whether this 'friend' of yours—"

"Oh my god, it was *not* me."

"—managed to win the competition after all, or whether this is a cautionary tale of tequila and over-confidence."

"Nope. I am officially putting a per-day cap on surfing stories. You'll have to wait until tomorrow night."

I like the way he says "tomorrow night" rather than just "tomorrow." Like he expects we'll be out on our trailer steps again, chatting away. Like maybe he's looking forward to it.

"Now it's your turn," he says. "Tell me something exciting about the life of Kim Watterson."

"Exciting?" My brow furrows. Despite being a movie star, there is very little about my life that could be described as exciting, and I've already shared all my best stories about my time on *Spy High*. "I had a fascinating phone call with my mom today about the trouble she's having giving Chandler Bing his suppositories."

Blake blinks.

"Chandler Bing is my dog," I clarify, realizing that I have never told him this.

"Ah. That makes a lot more sense than your mom personally attending to Matthew Perry's ass medication needs."

I laugh, and he grins again.

"So is this the dog that has three legs?" he asks. I've told him that much about my little Jack Russell terrier, even if I apparently left out his name.

"Yep."

"And you have other pets too, yeah?"

I nod. "Right now, I've got a bunny named Gunther and a cat named Janice. Well, Janice the Second, really. I had a hamster named Janice a few years ago. She only lived a few weeks, though, and it seemed like a shame not to reuse the name."

"*Friends* does make for a gold mine of pet names."

I smile. I love that show, even if some aspects of it don't hold up so well anymore. I always secretly wished I could be Phoebe—fun and free and weird in a way she embraced whole-heartedly. Really, though, watching her break social norms never failed to make me anxious.

I'm clearly a Monica.

I find myself wondering whether someone like Blake—not a Phoebe, for sure, but definitely not some neurotic, rigid rule-follower—would ever want to be with someone like me.

Not that it matters, my growing crush aside. He's a co-star, and my rules are in place for a reason.

"So do all these animals have missing limbs, or is it just Chandler Bing?" He's kidding when he asks this, but it's not far from the truth.

"Not missing limbs, no," I say. "But they all have special needs."

"Really?"

"Yeah. I love animals in general, but I'm a total sucker for the ones that need extra care. It's harder for rescues to find homes for them, you know? Because it can be a lot more work, and I totally get that not everyone has the time or means for that. But I do, and it's incredible to see how they thrive with a little love and attention." I blush, because I realize I barely took a breath between those sentences. I get carried away when it comes to my animals, much more than Blake with his surfing stories.

Blake doesn't seem like he minds. "That's awesome," he says with a soft smile.

"Well, my parents think it's less so when they have to take care of them when I'm away," I say with a chuckle. "They're just lucky there's not more. I have to keep myself from looking at rescue sites too often, or I'll adopt every animal I come across."

"Would that be so much of a problem? Kim Watterson single-handedly saves all the animals of the world?" There's a teasing note in his voice, but it's gentle.

I suck in my lips, then decide to tell him something I don't usually tell people. Not because it's embarrassing, but because it's so close to my heart, it feels like giving someone a piece of me—and I don't feel comfortable doing that very often. "My dream is to someday have a rescue of my own. Like, get this big plot of land and have the space to take in as many animals as I can. A place where they can live out their lives and get all the help they need. I know it would be too much for me to run all by myself, so I'd need to hire a staff, but I want to be hands-on, not just in this oversight role. I want to get to be there for each and every one."

Blake is just watching me, and in the pause that follows, I start to think that maybe I shared too much, maybe he knows that I don't do that and is wondering why on earth I would with him when we're clearly just friends—I made sure to be very clear on that point on day one—and I've made him uncomfortable.

But then he smiles again. "I can totally see it. You'd be incredible at that."

Warmth floods through me. He's not just saying that, I can tell. He's such a genuine, sincere person—it's one of the main things that draws me to him.

"Do you have any pets?" I ask.

He shakes his head. "We had a family dog growing up, but

I've never had a pet of my own." He pauses. "I've always wanted a pig, though."

I laugh, delighted at the thought of Blake Pless owning a pig. "Really?"

"Yeah. Like, a house pig. I always thought that would be amazing. I have no idea why."

"Because it *would* be amazing. You should totally get a pig."

He grins. "Maybe I will. Someday. If I can ever afford to not rent, because I doubt there's a landlord alive who would allow a pig as a pet."

"If you can ever afford it? You're a movie star now."

His smile slips, and I wonder if I said something wrong. "I'm in *a* movie. Star seems like a stretch."

I'm tempted to inform him that a leading role in a big-budget movie (for a rom-com, that is) opposite a well-known actress is more than what most people require to consider someone a movie star, but I don't want to seem like I'm full of myself. "So do you think by your next leading role you'll have earned the title?"

He makes a dismissive noise. "You assume I'll have one."

"You don't think you will?"

Blake shrugs. "I think I fell into this career by accident. It's probably not the smartest thing to assume I'll stumble into another film at all, let alone a leading role. Luckily, I still have that prime surf shop job to fall back on." He says this jokingly, but there's an underlying discomfort.

"You know you're really good, right?"

His eyes dart up to me, almost hopeful, but then he rolls them dramatically. "Oh, come on. You don't have to say that."

"I mean it. You are."

"If you mean I manage to say my lines and act like a human being, then yeah, I suppose I am a good actor."

I shoot him a hard look. "Thank you for reducing my lifelong profession to that."

The self-conscious smirk disappears, replaced by an even more self-conscious grimace. "No, I didn't mean . . . God, that was an asshole thing to say. I know there's a ton more to acting, that real actors have training and—"

"I was kidding," I say with a laugh. "I know what you meant. But I'm not kidding about the fact that you have natural talent."

He wets his lips. "You think so? I mean, I'm not a professional like you or anything."

"You're getting paid actual money for this movie, right? Because if all you're getting is free food at craft services, then I think you need a new agent."

"I'm also getting the chance to hang out with Kim Watterson, so—"

I groan and he smiles.

"But yes," he continues, "I'm getting paid, Miss Technicality. What I mean is, you have all this experience and skill, and I'm here due to a stroke of luck and a good agent."

"I do have lots of experience and skill," I say. The first is straight-up undeniable, given that I've been acting since I was a toddler, and the second, well—I'm good at what I do, and while I don't like to brag, I am proud of it. "Which means I know when other people have talent. And you do. You may not have all the training in the world, but you have really great instincts. Anyone can get the training and experience, and that's important over time. But those instincts are much harder to learn."

He watches me for a long moment. "Thank you. That means a lot, coming from you."

I hear the sound of voices in the distance, the first ones we've heard in a while, since most sane people who have to wake up at the ass-crack of dawn are asleep by now. We both look in that direction, but the voices quickly fade away as whoever it is disappears into their own trailer.

"You know," he says, "I might need to record you saying that for the next time I see my family. Kim Watterson thinks I have natural talent and good instincts. My mom and sister would be very impressed."

He says this offhandedly, but I don't miss the omission. "Not your dad? He wasn't a big *Spy High* fan?"

Blake rolls his eyes again, but not as dramatically as before. "He's not a fan of acting as a career choice. Calls it a 'dead-end job.' I think he was pretty ticked when I landed this role, because it would only encourage me in my terrible life choices." He laughs like it doesn't bother him, but I don't think for a second that's true. How could it not bother him? I'm pissed on his behalf.

"Does he really say that stuff to you?"

Blake shrugs, another dismissive gesture, but I notice how he's picking at a thread on the hem of his shorts. "Yeah. It kind of sucks. I get it, though. He always wanted me to have a practical, responsible job, but not a blue-collar one like he does. He wanted me to go to college, like that was the be-all, end-all. But I was terrible in school."

"Because of your dyslexia." I remember him on the boat that first day, studying the updated lines. I also remember being impressed that he was so open about that; a lot of people in this industry wouldn't be, for fear of showing some kind of weakness, even though it's anything but.

He nods. "Yeah. I didn't get diagnosed until I was fourteen. So for the longest time, he thought I didn't take things seriously enough, that I didn't focus. My teachers thought I had ADHD, but it turns out I didn't. By the time I got the actual diagnosis . . ." He looks down at his hands and his fingers go still. "I mean, I was a fourteen-year-old who could barely read. So I think it was safe for all of us to assume that college wasn't in my future."

My heart cracks open. I've noticed before how he deflects compliments, how often he self-deprecates. With some people, that kind of thing can be false humility, but I never get that sense with him. "That must have been difficult enough without your dad making you feel worse about it." Still making him feel worse about it, apparently. "If you wanted to go to college, though, I'm sure you still could. *And* keep acting."

"Eh." He wrinkles his nose. "College doesn't appeal to me,

19

anyway. I know I'm not book smart—it's kind of hard to be when reading is miserable."

I get the feeling that this isn't stuff he opens up about to a lot of people, at least not in this more serious way, and it feels incredible that he's able to be that way with me. "I think if you really want a long-term career in film, you'll be able to do it. And maybe when you're Megastar Blake Pless, your dad will finally have to admit that it's not such a dead-end job, and you're really great at it."

"I don't think he'd admit that even then," Blake says.

"Well, he can be wrong."

Blake's smile is both gentle and bright like the sun, all at once. "I'm guessing Kim Watterson very rarely is."

I grin at him. "It's both a gift and a burden."

He puts his elbows on the step behind him and leans back. I can't help but notice how his shirt clings to his chest—not too tight, like he's showing off, but just enough that I can tell there's some nice definition underneath. Definition I'll be feeling next week when we film our sex scene.

That image sends a flare of heat through me.

"I'll have to take your word for it," he says. "So I'm guessing your parents are pretty supportive of your career? They must be, since you were a child star. And since they're willing to give your dogs suppositories while you're away filming."

"They are," I say, tearing my gaze away from his chest. "Not the kind of crazy showbiz parents you hear about, who are willing to do anything to get their kid into the business and keep them there. They obviously got me into it in the first place, since I started when I was practically a baby. But it was always clear as I was growing up that it wasn't something I needed to keep doing if I didn't want it. They also made sure I knew all about the pitfalls and drawbacks and responsibilities of stardom, so I didn't go into it with a rosy view of fame."

"So you really love it, then," he says. "Not the fame, but the actual acting."

"Hey, I'm not knocking the fame, either. I get unlimited free veggie burgers at the sandwich shop on the Paramount Studio lot, sooo . . ."

"If all you're getting out of this is free veggie burgers, I think you need a new agent."

I laugh. He manages to make me do that more than pretty much anyone else. "Maybe. But yeah, I do love it." I pause. "Most of the time."

He tilts his head. "Most of the time?"

Now I'm the one shifting uncomfortably. It always seems so ungrateful to complain about being a successful actress, something so many people work for their whole lives and never achieve. "It can be a little isolating at times," I admit. "People don't treat you like you're a normal person. It can feel like either you're on this pedestal or you're competition." Neither of which I've ever felt from Blake, even if he was clearly a little awestruck by me that first day. That seems to have worn off, and besides, he was able to clap back about my candy preferences more or less instantly.

He frowns. "Yeah, I can see that. I haven't felt the competition thing from people yet, but even friends I've had forever have been acting weird around me since that first movie, and especially since I got this part. It must be a lot worse for you. It's always been this way, huh?"

"Not with everyone," I say quickly, lest he think I have *no* friends, which is not true. But I don't think stating that so emphatically is going to help my case. "And being on a pedestal or being competition is better than the other, too-common alternative—being the train-wreck former teen star who appears in tabloids for urinating in the champagne fountain at an Emmys after-party."

His eyes widen. "That is very specific."

"Yeah, well, I saw it myself, and I have never recovered. Fortunately, long before then, I'd already made the decision to take the career seriously, to be responsible to the projects I'm working on and the people I'm working with. And I owe so much of that to my parents. They could be over-protective, but they helped me come up with rules to avoid those traps. No drugs, no excessive partying—"

"No sleeping with co-stars." He says this with a teasing smile.

I flush all over, in a very different way than when I was thinking of him naked. I'm so embarrassed at how I practically beat him over the head with that stick the first day, especially now that I'm pretty sure he was misguided but not actually hitting on me. In my defense, I've had no small number of co-stars make obnoxious attempts to get into my pants on day one of filming, so I might be a little quick to judge anything that sounds like a line. "The rule is technically no *dating* co-stars, but . . . yeah."

There's a beat of silence which feels way more loaded to me than it undoubtedly is to him, and I suddenly feel the need to fill it, to explain myself. "It's a good rule, though. When I was younger, it was more about how actors can get so caught up in these on-set romances that they get distracted from the actual work. But since then, I've seen so many people get confused and think they're feeling things for their fellow actors that they're really not, you know? Like, because the characters are in love, and you're being these characters, it's easy to get that mixed up with real life. You know?" It occurs to me that I said "you know?" twice in that long, rambling diatribe, and that I probably sound like an idiot. For many reasons.

Blake picks at the thread on his shorts again. "Yeah, that makes sense."

It does, even though I've never before actually thought I had feelings for any of my co-stars, no matter how deep my characters' feelings were.

Maybe the rule makes even more sense now that I think I do. Now that I'm starting to regret, for the first time, having that rule at all.

There's a longer beat of silence, and now I'm feeling doubly embarrassed, and like I should never again entertain the idea that I might be a socially functional person. But then Blake looks back over at me, his lips tugging up, and I smile back.

There's too much about him that makes me want to smile. Too much about him that makes me want to sit out here and talk with him, just like this, nonstop.

And that's what finally compels me to say that I should probably get to bed.

"Yeah, me too," he says. Does he sound a little reluctant about that, or is it just in my head? "I know this isn't a thing for you, but *some* of us need our beauty sleep."

I shake my head. "Trust me, it's definitely a thing for me. Besides, my ass is getting numb."

I realize the moment those words leave my mouth that I've set myself up for a line about how there are some good ways to wake it up—a line I no doubt would have gotten from numerous co-stars in the past. But if Blake's thinking it, he doesn't say it.

I hate how much I hope he's thinking it.

"'Night, Kim," he says.

"'Night, Blake," I say back.

Then we both go into our trailers, and I spend way too long afterward lying awake and trying not to think about him.

THREE

Kim and Blake

Another week passes in a blur. An intense, sexually-frustrated blur.

Blake and I have spent every night sitting and talking between our trailers, and each day, I want more and more to invite him inside to spend some quality time between my legs.

Not that Blake has made one single overture about wanting that. He's been nothing but kind and professional, refusing even the most obvious opportunities for innuendo (even though I'm sure he's not missing them) and never saying or doing anything that might pass for hitting on me.

Though I *have* found a couple of suspicious peanut butter M&Ms in my candy mix. I'm sure he's sneaking them in there, though he vehemently denies it. That could be flirtatious, though it could also be friendly teasing, and I'm getting increasingly concerned that might be all we are.

Friends.

I can't blame Blake for sticking me in the friend zone, though. Really, I stuck myself there that first day we met.

I've been a bundle of regret and anticipation the closer we got to the filming the big sex scene, and now that day is here and I'm bursting with nerves. It's not the filming I'm worried about—well, not what I'm *mostly* worried about.

Last night while I was lying in bed, trying not to imagine what it would feel like if Blake were lying there with his arms around me, his hand working its way up my thigh—and then finally letting myself do some serious imagining of that while I worked out my frustration—I made a decision. An important decision.

Tonight I'm going to break one of my most steadfast rules. I'm going to sleep with Blake. If he wants to, that is.

God, I hope he wants to. Heaven knows I do. But what I'm feeling goes beyond sexual longing.

How far beyond is what I need to figure out.

I shift in the folding chair, smoothing out my sundress, even though it's about to get seriously wrinkled very soon. Techs and PAs and other crew members are running around, getting things set up, repositioning lights and cameras, shifting potted plants an inch to the right.

I've been in this business most of my life, so the typical pre-shooting chaos is generally comforting to me. Other than the first scene of any project, which is always nerve-wracking, and well . . . today.

I pop a few M&Ms in my mouth—two plain and one peanut. The perfect bite of the perfect candy mix. I know it's stupid—superstition, a good luck charm, something like that—but it makes me feel more confident that the scene will go well.

I bite into a peanut butter M&M, and my heart skips a beat. Normally, I would take any variance in my perfect mix as a bad omen, but today, I think it might be a good one.

I really, really want this scene to go well, though it's alarming how little of my thoughts right now can be spared for the film. And how very many of them are about the guy who just stepped out of hair and makeup, wearing a fluffy robe over a button-up shirt and no pants.

My blood heats up just from seeing Blake—okay, the not wearing any pants thing may contribute to that—but I try to

25

cover it with a friendly wave.

He smiles back, and god, that smile. Blake Pless is gorgeous, even by Hollywood standards. But it's not just how incredibly good-looking he is. I've worked with lots of gorgeous guys. I've done loads of kissing scenes and a handful of sex scenes.

None of those guys ever made me feel the way he does. None of them ever kept me awake at night, replaying every conversation in my head, smiling to myself at remembered jokes. Wishing we could just keep sitting outside our trailers all night, talking and laughing. Wishing I could kiss him as Kim kissing Blake and not as Alice kissing Tyler.

I'm becoming more certain every day that the things I feel aren't coming from Alice at all. That they're something deeper and more true than anything I've ever felt before.

It terrifies me that I have no idea if Blake feels the same.

I show up for work on the day we're filming my first-ever sex scene, and I'm nervous as hell. Not just because I somehow have to act like I'm having sex in front of camera techs and props people and makeup artists, but because I have to do all this with Kim Watterson.

Mercifully, I get to makeup without running into Kim, and they've got us in different makeup rooms today, with different techs, for reasons I assume are about to become obvious. Because today, after I get my face makeup done and my hair gelled in a way that looks natural but is actually unnatural as hell, the first instruction I'm given is to take off my clothes.

Which I do, and stand there like a mannequin while makeup people tape on the modesty pouch—an item alarmingly similar to a nude-colored sock—and then proceed to bronze and buff and apply concealer to every part of my body, including my ass.

It has never occurred to me before that there might be anything on my ass that needs concealing—maybe I should look

26

at it in a mirror more often. But then I'm given a robe and sent over to wardrobe.

I'm not wearing pants for the scene, apparently—too much effort to get out of when they're planning to shoot us from the waist up while our clothes are on—but they do give me a big fluffy robe to wear over my tight-fitting button-up shirt and otherwise nothing at all before I'm ushered out to the set.

We're having sex on a lounge chair on the patio outside the house where Kim's character is living for the summer. The set is already together, and crews are adjusting cameras set up above and around the lounge chair in question. Kim is already there, sitting in a folding chair, eating her perfect mix of M&Ms and wearing a sundress so thin that I bet it feels like nothing. She waves at me casually, but I can tell from her smile that she's nervous too.

I want to believe that's because she has as big a crush on me as I do on her. We've been flirting like crazy over the last two weeks, sitting on the steps between our trailers and talking until late into the night. (And yeah, okay, I've been up even later into the night relieving some pressure while thinking about her laugh, her smile, the sexy way she looks at me when the cameras are rolling and all the sexier things I wish she'd sneak into my trailer and do to me. I'm only human, after all.) We couldn't come from more different backgrounds, but somehow Kim seems to understand me better than anyone I've ever met.

Which is how I know I'm falling for her, hard.

Kim reclines in her chair, waiting for the scene to start. Her dress is short, not even reaching mid-thigh, and I'm aware that I'm hardcore checking her out as I wander over to her chair, but I can't help it. I'm grateful for the largeness and fluffiness of my robe, because I'm having all kinds of reactions that aren't exactly hidden by having a sock taped to my dick.

Act cool, I tell myself. We're filming all the exterior scenes around this house, but the interior ones will be filmed back at the studio in LA. Because the area isn't far off the road, the film crews have secured the perimeter with giant curtains hanging from metal rods that are sometimes used to erect green screens.

"Ironic, isn't it?" I say.

Kim gives me a hesitant smile. "What?"

"That they're so concerned about anyone seeing us when we're about to be filmed with the hope that millions of people are going to pay money to see our bare asses."

She laughs. "Yeah, well, you know what they say. Why buy the cow when you can get the milk for free?"

"I'm pretty sure that isn't about sex scenes."

She digs around in her M&Ms in the way that she does when she's not sure what to say. I've picked up on a lot of her little habits and tics over these last weeks. We've been together for almost every waking moment. "I found another peanut butter one in here today," she says. "You didn't happen to see anyone get close enough to pollute my perfect ratio, did you?"

"Damn. Maybe this film set *isn't* secure." I shake my head sadly. "Or maybe the manufacturer isn't as careful as they should be with their batches. You should write them a strongly worded letter."

"I *should.*" She gives me a knowing smile.

Kim knows perfectly well I've been parceling out a bag of peanut butter M&Ms into her candy bowl for more than a week. She hasn't quite called me on it, so I'm confident this was the right call. It's flirtatious without being obvious, which is a delicate line to walk, but one I'm toeing with precision.

I'm really not looking to bring on another lecture about how she'll never, ever, *ever* sleep with me. That stung the first day I met her, and I can only imagine how much it's going to hurt next time she feels the need to remind me. It won't matter that I'm into her and not her character. Alice is the only iteration of Kim I have a chance with, and that's only because it's written into the script.

The AD calls out to us. "All right. Kim and Blake, we're ready for you."

Blake's smile is the slightest bit hesitant. This is his first sex scene, after all. Given that, he's actually holding it together really well. I was a wreck before my first big sex scene, though since in that movie I was playing a crack-addled prostitute, that probably worked in my favor.

I wonder if he's nervous about doing this with me, specifically. If he's worried about our friendship—which is something I have never formed so deeply or quickly with another co-star before—changing after this.

I wonder if there's part of him that really wants it to, like I do. I head over to the lounge chair where we'll be filming the scene, and Blake follows behind me.

The director leans out from behind the monitors. "Let's get Blake lying down on the chair."

Blake obliges, and as his robe rides up when the director tells him to fold his arms behind his head, I can see the lean muscles of his inner thigh, and a little birthmark that I long to trace with my finger.

Or maybe my tongue.

I let out a breath, slowly. Controlled, so no one notices.

"Yeah, just like that," Derek continues, still talking to Blake. "But lose the robe, would you? You're not Hugh Hefner."

I stifle a smile at that, and especially at the way his cheeks flush as he tugs off his robe, and Julie from wardrobe advises him to put the robe over his lap for this shot. But not before I got a good glimpse of him in only the cock sock, which may cover things, but doesn't exactly hide the general (and generous) size or state of arousal—and now my cheeks are the ones burning. He looks up at me, and I look away, hoping he didn't see me checking him out.

Or maybe I want him to see, so he's not surprised when I proposition him later tonight.

I haven't quite decided on this point yet when Derek starts

with the directions again. "All right, Kim, when the shot starts, I want you to count to three, and then you're going to crawl up him. Keep your eyes on Blake's and keep crawling until you're right there. Then you guys kiss, and Kim, your hands are in Blake's hair, and Blake, you run yours up her back. Got it?"

Oh, I've got it.

The AD calls "action," the set goes still, and all I can hear is the pounding of my heart, the three count going in my head. Then I get down on the lounge chair with my knees on either side of his legs and begin crawling up him, feeling the skin of his legs warm against mine. Closer and closer, until our faces are inches apart, and god, his eyes are so bright, this blue-green that right now is tending more toward blue. His lips part, and I think his breath catches.

Or maybe it's just Tyler's that does, not Blake's.

Maybe I need to not confuse the two, maybe—

He leans up and his lips meet mine. We're kissing, and my whole body lights up, especially as his hands move along my body, as I can feel him even beneath that damn fluffy robe, and our kisses grow deeper, hungrier—

"All right, good." Derek's voice manages to register, thanks to the part of my brain that is still desperately trying to remember that this is a scene for a movie, being filmed in front of, like, a hundred people. The part of my brain that knows that sex scenes are actually super *not* sexy to film.

Or they never have been before.

"Keep kissing," Derek says, a direction I have no trouble following through with. "A little more passion, guys."

More passion? God, I'm already on fire with wanting him, how can it get more—

Blake pulls me closer, pressing my hips tighter against his, and Derek calls out, "Yeah, like that. Good."

Oh. Okay, yeah, that'll do it.

30

Kim is lying on top of me, and I'm sure she can tell exactly how excited I am, but she doesn't pull back, doesn't communicate anything other than this desperate desire for me.

No, for Tyler. Alice wants Tyler. Kim's right, we can't confuse ourselves with our characters. I try to focus on Tyler, on how much he's been longing for this, but in this case, I think Tyler and I are one in our desires. Kim and I are making out like brand new lovers, and it's the easiest acting job I've ever had. Being with Kim feels so natural, even if it's tempered by this sinking feeling, this deep, gut knowledge that this isn't real, not for her. It's just for the camera. When the director yells cut, it's all going to be over.

"Cut! That was good, guys. Let's get it again."

Okay, so maybe not the first time he yells cut.

Oh, god. We're going to do this again. How many takes are we going to do? I at once want to make out with Kim all day long and also need this to be over so I can beat off in my trailer and try to remember that it was all just pretend.

Keep it together, Blake, I tell myself. Of course it's pretend. We're *actors.* I can't help the way my body is reacting, but in every other way, I have to be professional. Kim will expect nothing less.

Kim stands at the end of the lounge chair, and I'm staring into the cool, blue eyes of the most gorgeous woman ever. I see hunger there, and she's not even on camera yet, but it doesn't mean anything. I try to relax, but as she crawls over me, my body tenses like a rubber band stretched near to breaking, and as our mouths meet, my whole body seems to exhale. Kim kisses me slowly and deeply, taking more charge this time, and I love it. I love everything about her; she's determined, beautiful, funny, scary smart—basically everything anyone could want in a woman.

Work it, I tell myself. Right now she's in my arms, and I'm supposed to be emoting all the things I'm feeling. I have no idea if I am, but I'm definitely kissing her and kissing her, and—

"Now Kim, unbutton Blake's shirt. One at a time, and use

both hands."

Kim's hand runs up my chest and lingers there for a moment. Then she begins working on the buttons, running her fingers over my skin between each one. I gasp and lean back, and she kisses my throat as she slips the shirt off over my shoulders.

"Blake, lift Kim's dress over her head. Then stop and look at each other for a three count. After that, Blake, you check her out, then unhook her bra."

I breathe, telling myself this is just another set direction and not a really good description of some of the fantasies I've had over the last two weeks. My heart is racing, and I'm worried I'm getting more flushed than they want me to be, but no one calls for makeup. I reach down, careful not to feel her up below the waist, as I know that's not in the shot, but as I pull the dress up past her hips, my fingers skim inadvertently over the strings of her thong. I move higher, finally able to run my hands gently along her soft skin as she lifts her arms over her head and the dress pulls free.

I feel this burst of shame amidst all the other body rushes I'm having. Kim is just doing her job. We're just working, and I'm way too into this. She's got to be able to tell, and I don't want to be this co-star she goes back to her girlfriends and complains about. This desperate newbie who thinks he could have half a chance with her, who made the scene so uncomfortable to film. I know better than to make advances she's already told me are unwelcome, but right now it's my job to express how much my character wants her, and I'm hardly an actor at all, let alone a seasoned professional, so she can probably tell—

"All right. Go for the bra, Blake. Any time now."

Shit. I drop my eyes to Kim's breasts—god, those breasts, they're perfect—then reach around and unhook her bra.

"Cut," Derek says. "You're checking her out, but don't just stare at her breasts. Your character is not a twelve-year-old boy. Keep those eyeballs moving, and look up at her again before you unhook her bra, okay?"

"Got it," I say, though my cheeks are burning, and Kim is straddling my lap, pressed all up against me, no doubt feeling every inch of how hard I am for her.

Yeah, I am definitely that desperate newbie, and I hate myself for it.

I can see Blake is embarrassed—and who wouldn't be, after that criticism from the director? But I can't break my eyes away from his. Pretty much since the day we've met, I've barely been able to do anything *but* look at him. Or think about him. Or look forward to when I get to talk to him again.

Is this what love feels like?

My throat closes up.

No, I tell myself. *Don't think that way, not now*. What's happening now is just a scene we're filming, and Blake is an actor, a really good one. Maybe he does like me as more than a friend, and I need to figure out how deep my feelings for him go, but this, right here, this is just acting. This is just us doing our jobs.

Isn't it?

"You okay?" I ask, trying to give him a sympathetic smile. Trying to act like the professional and not like a girl straddling a guy she might be in love with, and is definitely wishing she was doing a lot more with.

"Yeah," he says quickly. "You?"

"Yeah, fine." I hope he doesn't notice how out of breath I am. Or do I? I still can't decide whether I want him to know or not. Whether I want him to think I'm just being Alice or whether I want him to know that I'm not acting at all, that I can barely remember who the hell Alice Stone is when I'm with him like this.

This. This confusion right here is why I'm not supposed to date co-stars.

This, and the very real possibility that even if my feelings are real, and not some transference from my character, his—if he even has them—may not be.

I want so badly for him to want *me*. Not Alice. Not just a hot actress who turns him on during a steamy scene.

Me.

We hold this position while makeup comes in and adds a touch of powder here and there, and I try not to move too much. Then we're filming again, and Blake looks slowly down my body and back up, and I can feel my skin tingle under his gaze.

"Better!" Derek yells. "Now the bra."

I'm starting to feel resentful of the constant interruptions, because they remind me that this isn't Blake and me, and we aren't alone, and this isn't real. But I sure don't mind when Blake unhooks my bra and it falls free. Now I'm completely *topless* and straddling his lap, and the way he's looking at me is making my mouth go dry and other parts of me very much the opposite.

I wonder if he can tell what I'm thinking, if I've practically got a sign on my forehead: *I want to sleep with you, Blake. I want to know if I really am falling in love with you, and I'm going to ask if you want to have sex with me tonight, because I think that will help me know if this is real. And also because I've been fantasizing about you every night and I want it to be your hand between my legs instead of mine.*

If all that is on my forehead, it's got to be a pretty small font.

O h my god, Kim's lying on top of me in nothing but a thong. I'm afraid I'm about to make a mess for the makeup people to mop up, though I suppose at least it would be contained by the sock.

"Great," Derek says. "Now Blake, you're going to sit up, and Kim, you're going to wrap your legs around him."

We do, and Derek immediately yells, "Cut!"

I'm afraid it's because a certain modesty-pouch-covered part of me is poking obviously up into the shot, but this, while possibly true, is apparently not the problem. "Hold that pose, you two. Let's get the shot clear."

The makeup and props people start sweeping over us. One of them tugs my robe out from under Kim, and then she and I are pressed up against each other with nothing but my privacy bag and her thong between us. I notice now that the straps on her thong are sheer, so they'll be easy to edit out of shot. I'm guessing she'll be keeping that on.

Kim is still posed on top of me, somehow managing to maintain an even amount of pressure, so that she's neither pulling away nor leaning into me.

I guess I can add balance to her list of incredible skills. If we have to hold this position much longer, I'm going to be adding superhuman restraint to mine.

"You two are going to kiss passionately, while we take some different angles. Don't stop until I call it. Action."

Kim and I lock together, holding each other, kissing and kissing, our tongues brushing. She lets out a little gasp as I pull her closer, her breasts pressing tight against me, and even though I know they aren't using the audio from this, I groan. Her hands are in my hair again, and all I want to do is take her back to my trailer and make love to her and then hold her after and—

"Good, we got it. Okay, Blake, I want you to sweep Kim up in your arms and then lay her across the chair—switching so you're on top."

It's moments like this when I feel like I should get some training in dance just to have the first clue how to do a maneuver like that. I lift Kim, rocking up onto my knees, and throw off the balance of the chair. It tips up, and Kim shrieks and rocks back onto the chair. The legs come down on the concrete—and the remainder of my dignity—with a loud thump.

"Show me that footage," Derek says, as I use my excellent acting skills to avoid curling up on the concrete in a fetal position and dying.

Kim smiles at me. "Don't feel bad. It's a complicated chair."

"Yeah," I say. "I don't think I have a license to operate this kind of machinery."

I want to laugh, make another joke, anything. Blake and I have never had trouble chatting between takes—if anything, getting us to shut up is more the problem. But neither of us says anything else now. Blake may be the sex-scene virgin, but the way my body is reacting to every touch, you'd think I was an *actual* virgin.

I definitely don't want to give him *that* impression.

But I'm too full of nerves to say anything, because I've read the script directions to this scene. Many times. Many, many times.

I know what happens next.

Derek tells us he can map the transition, and we'll go on. "Now, Kim," he says. "Sit on the end of the lounge chair and lean back into the shot. Blake, you're going to kiss her down her stomach, stopping just above her underwear. Kim, you're going to be really into this. Hold onto his hair, like he's working you up."

I think I *am* going to be really into this. Probably a little too much.

"No problem," I say, though it comes out strained, and I stifle a wince. When Derek calls for action, I lie back, the sun above bright even through my closed eyelids, and Blake begins teasing his lips lightly on my stomach, right above the line of my underwear. My body arches reflexively into him, the ache for him to move just a few inches lower so strong, that I let out a whimper, my fingers tightening in his hair. I can feel the light graze of his teeth on my skin, and all I want is for him to *move lower*, to actually be doing to me what the shot will make it look like Tyler is doing to Alice—

"Great," Derek says. "Now Blake, you're going to kiss your

36

way up her body, until you get to her shoulder, and then bring your right hand up and cup her breast."

Blake starts to move up, and though I wanted him going the opposite direction mere seconds ago, this feels amazing too, his hands wandering back up my sides, his lips lighting along my skin, up and up. His fingers gently sliding along the curve of my breast—

"Cup it, Blake!" Derek yells. "Cup it!"

Even as worked up as I am, I can't help but let out little giggle at this, and Blake laughs too. Derek tells us to back it up a bit and go again, and this time Blake goes for a more deliberate grab of my boob—which isn't quite as sexy as his previous move, but maybe looks better on camera?

Blake kisses up my neck, and I'm back in the zone again. Honestly, even the straight-up boob groping feels pretty damn good with him on top of me like this, and he's nibbling on my ear, which sends another wash of heat through me, and then—

"Cup it, Blake!" he whispers in my ear.

I nearly die trying not to laugh, but I manage.

It hits me then that as gorgeous as he is, as much as my body burns with his every touch, the way he can make me laugh may be the sexiest thing of all.

And that's a pretty damn high bar.

All right, you guys are starting to grind now, and Blake, you're inside her, and the passion is building. Makeup, give me some perspiration here. Make them look like they mean it."

Oh, god, I mean it. I'm trying as hard as I can *not* to seem like I mean it. Makeup spritzes us with a glycerin and rosewater mixture that is supposed to look like sweat on camera, and we start moving, because no one has yelled cut. We kiss again, and I let my mind wander over what it would feel like to really be inside her, trying to channel all that passion and emotion into Tyler. He's finally getting to be with the woman he loves, the girl he wants more than anything in the world, and if I'll never have the satisfaction of knowing what that's like, at least I can live it through him. I've had plenty of sex before, though the audience and stage directions are definitely new. But despite the intense awkwardness of *that*, our bodies move together naturally. Too naturally. I'm pretty sure that I am actually going to finish in the modesty shield and I'm wondering if that's going to freak Kim out or make her feel used.

I can't bear the thought of either of those possibilities.

With Blake moving against me like that, I am no longer Alice Stone. No, I'm definitely Kim, and all I can imagine is Blake being really inside me, and we're moving against each other, and I can feel it building up in me like this is actually happening. We're both letting out little gasps and moans, and if I thought my body was lit up before, now it's a like a stadium at night, and god, I want him so bad, want to break apart against him, break apart together, both of us, and—

"Cut! That looks great, guys. Put on your robes. We'll run through the footage, but I think we got it."

Blake pulls back and all but launches himself off me, and the sudden ache of him gone tugs an inadvertent groan from my throat.

"Sorry," he says, but doesn't look at me, which is good, because I'm probably ten shades of red, both from the groan—seriously, Kim?—and realizing how close I came to . . . well, coming. On camera. From dry humping, like I'm a teenager.

I have this sudden fear that he knows this, that maybe it made him super uncomfortable. That he could feel how wet I was—god, his face was inches away at one point, he must have known.

Blake still doesn't look back as he sits on a folding chair and takes a long sip from a bottled water.

A PA brings me a robe, which I pull on and tie around my waist, then go over to my own chair to try to get my pulse to finally slow back down and my body to stop loudly complaining about what it has been denied.

Maybe he liked it as much as I did, and that's why he jumped away so fast. Maybe he does want more with me.

Or maybe I'm in love with him, and it took me too long to figure that out—and too many protestations about how I never date co-stars—and I've been friend-zoned so hard that even filming a scene like this won't get me out of it.

Either way, I'm pretty sure I'm going to find out tonight.

FOUR

Blake

Kim and I agree to meet up later that night. We've been hanging out after filming, getting late night food at the local diners or ordering in, just to get something different from the food provided on set. We both agree that we need showers after all the body makeup and glycerin spray, and I need to do some post-filming relief under the hot water that I definitely don't want Kim to know about.

It helps, but only a little. As I dress and get ready to go meet Kim, my whole body still feels like it's vibrating. The experience of being so close to being with her . . .

It's maddening to now know everything from her scent to the feel of her skin against mine—and also to know that unless they discover they need pick-up takes, I'm never going to get there again.

I can't let Kim see how much that bothers me. We still have a lot of filming to do, both on location and back at the studio, and I'm not going to be the cause of set drama. Just because I can't keep my hormones under control is no reason to ruin a perfectly good working relationship.

Besides which, the stupid part of me is desperate to stay friends with her, to have that much intimacy with her at least, even if I know we won't keep up once the movie is over. Not in the same way we're connecting on set.

Kim meets me outside my trailer wearing a striped halter top and a tight denim skirt. She looks sexy whatever she wears, but the way the skirt hugs her hips has me thinking all kinds of impure thoughts as we walk over to where our driver will pick us up and take us somewhere to grab food. I'm aware of my body in a way that I'm usually not, attuned to exactly where I'm standing in relation to her, careful that our hands don't brush, that I don't seem like I'm hovering. What I want to do is sweep her into my arms and kiss her until we can't take it anymore and then go back to my trailer and strip off all our clothes and make love all night long. My mind is already working through all the possible things we could do to each other, all the things I want to feel and make her feel.

She's called for the driver already—a perk for the stars, apparently, is that we get to be chauffeured wherever we go. It seems a little weird to me, but I'm not going to bother renting my own car just to prove I can drive myself.

By the time we get in the car, I'm already nearly as worked up as I was after that scene. Kim is quiet, but she keeps smiling almost shyly at me, so I don't think she's aware of how I'm feeling—or if she is, she's just attributing it to the physical realities of what we did earlier.

We don't talk much on the way to the diner, which is unusual for us, even with a driver also in the car. I'm not used to having a hard time thinking of what to say when I'm with Kim. In fact, on set we're becoming known as the actors who never shut up, and I think sometimes the director leaves the camera rolling just so we don't start chatting between takes.

We head into the diner and order the usual—there are only so many diners in this small town, so while we try not to let our schedule be predictable, we're starting to have a usual at most places. Since Kim is Kim, the staff all know what it is.

"So," Kim says, leaning toward me across the table. "How

does it feel to have lost your sex-scene virginity?"

I laugh, but it sounds nervous even to me. "Good to have that out of the way, I suppose."

"If it helps," she says, "I'd never have known it was your first time." She's giving me this sexy smile, though I'm sure she doesn't mean it that way.

"You're just saying that."

"Never. The last time I did a scene like that, I think the guy had an entire onion for breakfast. And it *wasn't* his first time."

I fiddle with the dessert menu, which consists of two choices: ice cream sundae and "Lu-Lu's Famous Mud Pie."

"I certainly hope I rated higher than onion guy," I say.

Kim seems to be considering this.

"Seriously?" I ask.

She dissolves into giggles, and hers sound a bit nervous as well. "Yes, you definitely rank above onion guy."

"But still below someone," I say, mostly because I want her to tell me I'm the best on-screen lay she's ever had.

She shrugs. "Truth is, I don't have *that* much experience. I was on the Family Channel for a long time."

I refrain from asking how our heavy makeout compared to her real life experience. I'd rank it up with all but the very best sex I've ever had, and neither of us even got to finish.

My cheeks grow hot as I think about how much farther it went in my mind afterward in the shower.

"But hey," she says, "they got it in just a couple of takes, so I must not be the only one who thought you did a good job."

Right. Because how it looks on film is definitely what I should be worried about.

"Despite me apparently ogling you like a twelve-year-old boy."

"Well, the director was the one who was a *little* too excited about you pulling off my bra. I thought he was going to come over and do it for you."

"I know, right? And then him like, 'Cup it, Blake! No, *cup* it! CUP IT, Blake!' Like what every woman wants is to be honked like a fog horn."

Kim laughs so hard I think she might fall off her chair. "Yes, that's definitely on my top ten list of sexy maneuvers."

"Right up there with being flipped over in a guy's arms and having the chair flip with you."

She holds up one finger. "In your defense, I don't know how you were supposed to do that on a lounge chair without flipping the thing. It's not exactly the most sturdy of furniture. I think if we had sex on it for real, we'd probably have broken it."

Heat scorches through my body. Just the thought of us doing that—sneaking back onto the set, maybe, and making love on the chair, just to see if it would hold up . . .

If Kim wanted to do that, it would be well worth any chance we had of getting caught. And I'm sure we wouldn't be the first movie stars to reenact their sex scenes on the set furniture.

My fantasizing is interrupted by the waitress bringing over our food—a veggie burger for Kim and a regular cheeseburger for me. We take a few bites of our food in silence, and Kim twirls a french fry around in her ketchup. Somehow even this is sexy. I'm not sure it's possible for me to jerk off enough to make her less so. "Even though it's obviously pretend," she says, almost too casually, "it makes sense that scenes like that could wind someone up."

Gee, I wonder what she's referring to. I grimace at my plate. "Sorry about my um . . . reaction."

"Oh. No, you don't need to apologize. You weren't the only one having reactions."

I look up quickly. It's embarrassing how much I like hearing that. "Yeah?"

"Yeah," she says, in that still too-casual tone. "If you wanted, I was thinking maybe we could go back to my trailer and do that for real."

I break out in full-body goosebumps. She can't really be suggesting that. Can she? "What about your co-stars rule?"

She shrugs seductively. Or maybe she shrugs normally, but

she could probably be plucking a chicken and I'd find it suggestive right now. "I was thinking about making an exception."

My mouth goes dry. I want to be that exception. I want to take her back to our trailers and spend the rest of the night making a deeply compelling argument that she should make further exceptions for me in the future.

Except that the filming we did today worked her up, too, and I don't want to take advantage of her. "Don't you think you might regret that? You have those rules for a reason, right?"

Kim looks up at me, and our eyes lock like they did while we were filming, and I can't breathe. Kim is so beautiful, inside and out, and I know I'd never regret anything I did with her.

"Remind me what that reason was?" she asks.

Oh, god. I don't want to remind her. "You worry about getting your character's emotions confused with yours," I say. "You don't want to do anything impulsive."

One corner of her mouth turns up, and I find myself staring at her lips, remembering what it was like to feel them against mine. If she was kissing me for real—kissing *me*, not my character—I'm pretty sure I'd lose what little restraint I've managed to hold on to.

"Maybe it isn't impulsive," she says. "Maybe I planned this."

I swallow, and Kim smiles, like she can tell exactly what she's doing to me. "Planned what?" I ask.

"Maybe I decided before today that I wanted to sleep with you. And I thought tonight would be a good time to be spontaneous."

I laugh, even though it's definitely a wound-up laugh. That line of thinking is so classically Kim. "*Spontaneous*? You *planned* to be *spontaneous*?"

"What? I can't make a plan to seduce my super-hot co-star?"

She didn't need to. I was already thoroughly seduced. "*Spontaneously*," I say. "Do you even know what that word means?"

Kim laughs. "Well, it's spontaneous for me."

I believe that, and it's part of what worries me. "I just don't want you to regret it in the morning. I mean, what, tomorrow we'd go back to being just friends?"

She opens her mouth and closes it. Then she wets her lips. "Sure," she says carefully. "Nothing serious."

I pick up one of my own french fries, trying not to look disappointed. Of course she doesn't want to pursue anything. Which means we could have what I already know would be a night of phenomenal sex, but then tomorrow, everything would go back to the way it was.

I'm barely an actor. I don't have much in the way of skills beyond just standing there and being a guy who remembers his lines. I don't think I'll be able to keep acting like it's no big deal when I still have to spend every day with her as if nothing happened, as if I feel nothing more than friendship for her.

She toys with the straw in her water and the cubes clink around in the glass. "You don't want to. Which is fine. It was just an idea."

But I swear now *she* looks disappointed.

"It's not that I don't want to," I say. "Believe me, I do."

"Then what? You're the guy who wanted to 'rehearse' our kissing scene, so you can't tell me you have hang-ups about co-stars."

I groan. "Again, I really *did* want to rehearse. I was nervous as hell, and I thought if we ran through it once, I might not flub the scene when we did it for the cameras."

Kim looks suspicious. "And yet you did just fine."

"I guess. They made us do, like, fifty takes, so I don't know."

"That was because the wind kept blowing things around in the shot and making a wreck out of my hair."

We're getting off track now, and I'm both terrified and desperate to get back there.

"I just don't want to be a regret you have," I say. "Maybe you were right about the co-stars thing. Maybe it is easy to confuse your character's feelings for your own."

Kim stares down at her hands, which are now resting in her

lap. "Sure. Okay." She doesn't look okay, though. She looks hurt, and I hate that I did that to her.

"It's not a rejection," I say quickly. "But I care about you. I don't want to mess this up."

"Our friendship, you mean."

"Yeah," I tell her. "Because that's all you want, right? Casual. Like friends with benefits."

"Right," Kim says, and I nod, even though she's still not looking at me. I understood her right, and as much as my body hates me for it—and most of my mind as well—deep down I know I don't want to be a notch on Kim Watterson's bedpost. I don't want to finish filming and do publicity tours and attend the premiere, all with a constant knot in my gut from having been just a passing fling, just a fuck buddy.

I can't be that, not with her.

Kim has started very studiously picking the sesame seeds off the top of her bun—not usually a habit of hers—and I wish I was someone else, someone who could give her what she wants without getting all attached.

I'm trying to think of some way to say that without sounding completely pathetic, when she suddenly blurts out, "I mean, unless you *wanted* to date. If you did, that would be cool."

My mouth falls open, and Kim winces like she regrets this already.

"Really?" My voice cracks like I'm a teenager, and she looks up at me sharply.

God, I think it might just now be occurring to her that I'm into this idea, and I'm not sure how such a smart, observant woman can have missed something so obvious.

"Yeah." She bites her lower lip. "I mean, if you want to."

"I want to." More than she could possibly know.

"Date me?" she says, and I laugh.

"Yes, I want to date you."

"But not have sex with me."

Kim sounds impossibly confused, and I reach across the table

46

for her hand. "Both. Definitely both."

A slow smile creeps across her face. "Yeah?"

"If you're sure about breaking the rules."

"Like I said, I planned this." She grins. "To be *spontaneous*."

"You really need to look up the definition of that word."

Kim swats at me across the table, and I dodge and she knocks over my little paper cup of ketchup. She doesn't look sorry about it. Our eyes meet, and I'm swept up in joy and anticipation. Kim wants me. She wants to be with me tonight, and she wants to date me, and—

"Do you want to get out of here?" I ask.

"Absolutely," she says.

She doesn't seem any more concerned than I am about the fact that we have eaten very little of our dinner, and I'm thinking now that she, like me, may be far hungrier for other things. I pay the check, and Kim doesn't argue that we have to split it, like usual. We hold hands as we walk out into the parking lot, but we don't get any farther than the curb before I'm overcome with this desperate need. I spin her around to face me and hold her body against mine. I push her hair back over her ear, and Kim looks up at me, her eyes fixing on my lips.

Then I'm kissing her. Not Tyler kissing Alice but Blake kissing Kim, lifting her into my arms and kissing the hell out of her in the way I've wanted to since we first met. And as much as kissing her in front of the cameras got me going, it's nothing compared to how turned on I am now, how every neuron is firing, every cell in my body is humming, and the heat that's building between us feels like an inferno.

We break apart, breathing hard, and Kim groans softly.

I press my lips to her forehead. "Yeah?"

"Um, *yeah*."

We're both laughing and holding each other, and when the car arrives, we link arms and climb into the back seat. It's just a sedan, so there's no partition, but Kim and I still can't keep our hands to ourselves, and now I'm definitely not minding neither of us having to drive. I'm sliding my hand up her thigh, and she's letting her knee fall to the side, inviting my hand up farther. Her fingers tease the skin at the top of my waistband, sliding up under the edge of my shirt and circling over my skin, sending shivers through me. I want to slide my hand all the way up and inside her, but I'm not sure how she'd react to me finger fucking her in front of the driver—though I'm sure he's seen worse—and besides, I'm tired of us having an audience. What I want with her now is just between us, and it's not anyone else's business. I stop my fingers right at the edge of her underwear—not a thong this time—and Kim slips hers underneath my jeans and then back out again. The barest graze against me, and my eyelids flutter closed.

I bury my face in her hair and whisper against her ear. "Tease," I say.

"Mmm," she answers. "Just wait."

I wrap my arm around her and hold her against me, savoring the heat, the spicy-sweet tension buzzing between us. I massage the inside of her thigh, and I can feel her getting wet through her underwear.

I'm not the only one dying of anticipation.

FIVE

Kim and Blake

The drive from the diner back to the set seems to both pass in a second and take an eternity. My lips can still taste Blake's from when he kissed me—kissed *me*, not Alice—and I'm dizzy with the touch of his fingers on the inside of my thigh, massaging me just along the edge of my underwear.

God, I want this man. Deeply. Desperately.

And he wants me.

That makes me the most light-headed of all, I think. Not just that he wants to sleep with me, but that he doesn't want to *just* sleep with me. I gave him the opportunity, made sure he knew he didn't have to commit to anything more. That we could just go back to being friends afterward.

It was a cowardly move on my part, because I already knew I wanted more, despite this plan being what was supposed to tell me that. And when he said that maybe I was right, maybe it's easy to confuse character's feelings with your own, my stomach dropped down to my knees. If he thought he had any feelings before, he knew now that it really was only character transference, after all. That he cares about me, but not the way I really want him to.

There was something about the way he asked if I wanted to be friends with benefits, though, that led me to blurt out—in

49

last-ditch desperation—that we could date, if he wanted to. I was mostly sure he didn't, and that I was only putting my dignity out there to get stomped on right along with my heart.

But he wants to be with me. I saw that hope bright on his face, and my heart leapt right up into my throat.

Other parts of me had plenty of reactions, too. Just like they are now, feeling him warm against me, his fingers moving against my skin, tracing those gentle circles that are sending waves of goosebumps up and down my body. My hands are just under the edge of his shirt, doing the same to him just above his pants, feeling the tension of his muscles. His face is buried in my hair, and his breathing is shallow.

I'm seriously contemplating just asking the driver to pull over somewhere and leave us here alone for a good hour— damn, that would be a good hour—but we arrive at the set, and I have no idea how we're already here, how I barely noticed the entire ride back.

Blake grabs my hand, and we full-on run to my trailer. I'm so giddy with the thrill of this I want to laugh, but my heart is still up in my throat and anyway, there's a lot of things I want to do so much more than laugh right now. I can't wait any more—the second we're inside my trailer, I pull his shirt off, needing to feel more of him. Needing to feel him when it's just us and we're not being directed, and it's real, god, this is going to be real.

He has my shirt off so soon after that I think he's feeling the same way. His hands are on my ass, pulling me against him, and heat floods all my senses.

"Kim," he says, barely a breath. There's a desk lamp that I must have left on before I went out for dinner, and though it's not incredibly bright, I can see the hungry way he's looking at me. I'm about to whisper his name back, hoping he can read that same hunger for him, but before I can, his lips press against mine again, and I'm not sure I can remember *either* of our names.

Kim's hands are circling my waist, still teasing just underneath my waistband, and I want to shrug out of my jeans and give her full access, but I also desperately want her to be the one to undress me. We kiss and kiss, and I unhook her bra and pull it free. "Cup it, Blake," she says against my mouth, but neither of us are laughing now, and instead of cupping it, I run my thumb in circles around her nipple, eliciting shivers and moans. At last, her fingers work their way around to unbutton my jeans, and she slides her hands down inside my boxers.

I roll my head back as she handles me. Her fingers run up and down at just the right rhythm, and I've had orgasms that aren't half as pleasurable. "Oh, god," I moan, and Kim grins up at me.

"God has nothing to do with the things I'm going to do to you," she says, and I lean down and kiss her hard. My pants fall to the floor, my boxers along with them. Kim sheds her skirt and I kick off my shoes and step out of them and then lift her up into my arms, her legs wrapping tight around my waist. I'm seeing stars, but I carry her through the trailer and lie her back on her bed, and then start at her knees with my mouth, working slowly up and up, savoring the gasps and moans and the desperate way she says my name. I reach her underwear and ease them off, tasting how wet she is, how ready, and her whole body arches back as she gasps in pleasure.

It's all for me, and no one else.

That first kiss with Blake, that very first day, was already incredible. Kissing him on the lounge chair for our sex scene, feeling that sense of falling so deep, was even more so. Kissing him outside the diner, knowing that he really wants me, even better still.

Now, kissing him here, feeling the fire of everything we're so close to doing, is another step higher.

I wouldn't have thought it could keep getting better; I wouldn't have thought there was any better to go.

And I have a pretty strong feeling I'm not even at the pinnacle yet of where I can get with him. Blake's lips trail up the inside of my thighs, his hair tickling my skin.

I'm the one moaning now, my breath hitching, especially as he takes off my underwear and presses his lips right there between my legs. Everything in the world is centered right there, where his mouth is moving against me, where his tongue is flicking gently and then insistently.

I can't keep myself from arching and shaking and whimpering, and I'm guessing by the way my movements and sounds make him work me up even harder, he doesn't want me to stifle any of this. The pleasure is building and building, making my body shudder even before I'm there, because I can feel it so close, so close, and I'm gripping his shoulders and wanting more of him, more—

The searing heat overtakes me, and I cry out his name as I come apart for him. I'm weak, so deliciously weak, but as he kisses his way up me until his body is right on mine, that weakness becomes need all over again.

We kiss and kiss, and he tastes like sex and longing and, most of all, him. I've never used drugs before—I'm way too much of a rule-follower, and that has always been a big one—but being with him has to be better than any high.

I can see how it could be addictive, too, which is terrifying, but I'm lost in the throes of it now.

More. I need more of him.

We pull apart, and his eyes lock on mine, his breath heavy and fast. "Do we need a condom?" he asks.

I got some before today, once I decided on my plan, and I have them in my purse, but that feels so far away right now, and technically, we may not need them. "I'm clean and on the pill," I say. "So it really depends on you."

I don't normally trust a guy enough to make that call for me, but with Blake, I do, and it's not just because I'm so impatient to have him inside me.

I trust him.

I trust him, and I love him.

The thought is so strong, so deeply rooted in me, that it takes my breath away. And that's even before his lips part and he gives me one last, intense look of need and enters me.

Oh god, how he feels inside me.

I'm swept under the waves of him, I'm blinded by the sun of him, and it's all I ever want. I can hear myself whispering "yes" over and over and over again, but what I'm thinking—and what I'm afraid will actually escape my lips—is *I love you, I love you.* Then the delirious climax hits me again and I can't even manage a single word, just a wordless cry as I shake and shudder, this time fully against him.

But he's still there, still hard, and I can't stop, don't want to stop. Not before he comes too, not before I give him even a fraction of the pleasure he's given me. And from the sounds he's making, from the way his body is trembling, he's not far off.

I sit up, pulling back just enough to flip him over—something that's a lot easier to do in a bed than on a lounge chair. He has this stunned, dazed grin as I straddle him and ease him entirely inside me again. His eyes flutter closed and he groans and I begin riding him hard. It's a glorious view, being on top of Blake like this, leaning over him and holding tight to his taut shoulders, seeing the way his head tips back, the way his Adam's apple bobs with his moans, and it works me up all over again.

I've never come more than twice in a single round of sex before, but I'm feeling it building again, higher and higher.

My rhythm becomes faster, and his hands grip my hips, driving me down harder onto him, and he's shaking, his moans intensifying, and mine are too. I cry out his name, and he echoes with mine and his breath catches and I can feel his whole body tense and then quake, pulling me right over the edge with him, that blinding light enveloping us both.

Nothing has ever been like this.

No one has ever been like him.

In my entire life, nothing has ever turned me on as much as Kim screaming my name as she comes. My muscles seem to spasm as one, tightening and then letting go with the sweetest, most breathtaking release. Kim collapses on top of me, and I hold her tight against me. The sweat beading on our foreheads, glistening in our hair, is real this time, as is all of it, everything I feel for her, everything she is to me. I've never felt like this, not before sex and not after, and I know it's not just because I've never come like that, not ever in my life.

I'm in love with her, I realize. I'm in love with Kim.

I don't want this to end, not tomorrow, not when filming is over. Maybe not ever. I know better than to say that out loud, but I can't bear to not say *something*. "So," I say, when I catch my breath enough to speak, "how serious is this dating allowed to be?"

"I don't know." She's panting, and it's sexy as hell, and already starting to work me up all over again. "I guess it depends on how serious you feel."

"I could feel pretty serious. Girlfriend serious, maybe." I sound more doubtful of that than I am. I've had girlfriends before, and I'm not afraid of monogamy, but I've never felt this kind of desperate need for it before, like she's a craving I can't kick, an itch that will never be entirely scratched.

Or maybe, I think in a daze, *it's just that I'm in love.*

"Really?" Kim says.

"Yeah," I say too quickly, then unconvincingly add, "I mean, no pressure." I want to tell her how I feel, but I'm just too scared. I have to play it off as a joke. "But you must have noticed how desperately into you I am. I'm not that good an actor."

Kim smiles, and I don't think it's because she finds this funny.

"I was actually starting to be afraid I missed my chance and got friend-zoned."

I give her an incredulous look. "Um, no. Definitely not friend-zoned."

Kim laughs. "Apparently not. And I suppose if I'm in a movie with my boyfriend, then I'm not *really* breaking my co-star rule."

This feels like a very narrow technicality, but I'm sure as hell not going to complain. I run my lips along her jaw. "I don't mind being the exception to the rule."

"Mmm." Her body twists against mine like, despite having finished—I'm pretty sure—three times, she isn't done, not even a little. "I have a feeling you're going to be an exception to a lot of rules."

I hope to stay that way for a long, long time.

SIX

Kim

It takes about two weeks of us sneaking into each other's trailers at night (and out again in the morning before call time, to change and avoid the walk of shame) before our relationship goes from internet speculation to full-on, widespread confirmation. This comes in the form of us appearing in *People* magazine's "Heart Monitor," with a picture someone got of us on one of our breaks, leaning against the back of my trailer with me cuddled up under his arm, and him planting a kiss on the top of my head. I'm beaming so hard, I'm practically a floodlight.

The pic is labeled "Hot New Couple," which I can't disagree with. I'm just surprised it took so long for this to get out. We aren't exactly the most stealthy people in the world.

I don't mind it being out; it was going to at some point, and I'm happy that Blake and I can be more open. But the big downside to this—which was also inevitable, but which I was hoping to put off as long as possible—is that now my parents know. I've gotten three calls from them today, none of which I have picked up or returned.

It's ridiculous, I know. I am a grown woman who can date whoever she wants and who can make her own choices for her career.

But I know how proud they were of me for sticking to my years-long choice to not date a co-star. To not let myself get distracted from the job I'm here to do, not let something that's unlikely to be more than just an on-set romance take my focus away from giving the best performance I possibly can.

It's not like they're going to tell me I can't date Blake. But they're definitely going to be concerned and remind me of all the reasons I had this rule to begin with. Telling them that my feelings are real and Blake's are too, that this is more than just some emotional runoff from our characters, won't do any good. They might not say so outright, but they'll think that this is what everyone says, and I'm just being taken in by it all. They'll be disappointed in me, which I hate, and I won't be able to stop thinking about how they sacrificed so much to support my career, and how so much of this film's success depends on my performance, so many people depending on me, and—

I squeeze my eyes shut, trying to stop the thoughts that are circling faster and faster.

No. I'm going to show them and everyone else that I can have a real, true relationship with Blake and be the professional, hard-working actress I always am.

Focus on that, Kim.

Which is what I'm trying to do right now, sitting on the bed in my trailer with tomorrow's script pages spread out in front of me and a pack of multi-colored highlighters spilled out around them as I furiously mark the lines. I've got a purple highlighter—the most important color in my coded system—clenched between my teeth, because I've somehow lost the cap in the sheets. I'm only wearing a t-shirt and panties, and I've already managed to get a long purple streak across my inner thigh.

Normally by this time, Blake would already be here with me, but he's got a night scene to film. So for the last couple hours, it's just been me and my highlighters and script pages, trying my very best not to think about how me messing up this film could affect my career, could affect Blake's career, might make him regret being with me to begin with, might—

The trailer door opens and Blake walks in.

Thank god. Nothing distracts me from my worries better than that incredible smile of his.

A smile which stretches wider when he sees me.

"Wow," he says. "Every time I think you can't get sexier, you somehow manage it."

I grin back at him around the highlighter. I'm not sure how legitimately sexy I am at the moment, given that my hair is pulled up in a messy bun, and I have no makeup on and a big purple streak on my leg. I'm pretty sure he's joking, but I love hearing him say it anyway.

I take the highlighter out of my mouth to say, "Right back at you." I deliberately ogle him—never an unpleasant thing to do, especially with his fresh-from-the-shower wet hair and clinging t-shirt.

He laughs and flops down on the bed next to me, though just beyond the spread-out papers.

"How'd your scene go?" I ask.

He groans. "The only thing I had to do was jog down the beach and then stop and look out broodily at the ocean, but Derek had me do, like, thirty takes. Jog, stare broodily. Jog, stare broodily. There are only so many ways you can do these things."

"Oh, yeah. Those scenes are the worst, and for some reason, directors always want a billion takes. By about the tenth, I am no longer able to channel my character's thoughts and am instead thinking broodily about whether catering is going to have that Greek salad again soon."

"Exactly." He smiles over at me and trails his fingers up my bare leg, sending tingles all along my skin. "I might have been thinking broodily about how much I wished I was back here with you instead."

"You weren't the only one." I lean over to kiss him, which he returns eagerly, hungrily, and I'm starting to tangle my fingers in his hair, and the highlighter slips from my hand and—

"Shit," I say, pulling back to see the big purple splotch on my sheets behind him. "I really need to find that cap."

"Or you could, you know, just set it down somewhere *not* your bed." He glances over the papers. "Unless you think you can still find a word in there that isn't highlighted." His voice is gently teasing, but I can tell he thinks this markup is more intense than usual. Which it definitely is.

"You're probably right," I say, scooping up the highlighters and plopping them all on my nightstand. Several roll off, but I don't care. For as organized as I try to be in my schedules and actions, I'm actually not that much of a neat-freak. "It just . . . helps me feel like I really have this down." I gesture at the script, though I know it's about more than that. He's smart, so he's probably figured it out, too, that somehow highlighting the hell out of this script is an attempt to feel like I can handle life.

What I'm not ready to admit is the time last year that I could barely breathe around the panic when I found that my green marker had dried out, and I was fairly sure my world was going to fall apart.

Shit. I really need to find that cap.

He lays on his side, propping himself up on his elbow. "So," he says carefully. "Have you called your parents back yet?"

Yep, he's definitely figured it out. Which I guess means that's another quirk of mine which doesn't freak him out too much, so that's good.

"Not yet," I say. "I, um. I figured I'd finish up with this first."

"Makes sense." He toys with the edge of one of the script pages, frowning at it, and I wonder if it bothers him that I haven't told my parents yet. His family's known about us for about a week now, and his mom and sister are extremely excited about it. His dad, as Blake warned, doesn't seem to care much either way, wanting little to do with any part of Blake's acting "lifestyle."

Ugh.

I'm about to assure Blake that nothing my parents can say will keep me from wanting to be with him—if that's what he's worried about—but he breaks the silence first.

"I apologize ahead of time for Tyler being such a dick in tomorrow's scene," he says, holding up the page. "I mean, seriously. Can she really be in love with this guy?"

I hope he doesn't notice my flush. Not that Blake's at all a dick, but him saying that second part makes me think (again, because I've thought this a *lot* lately) about how I haven't told Blake yet that I'm in love with him, even though I've known since that day we first slept together.

I'm scared of putting him in a position of having to tell me he's not there yet. I know he's in this, but it's still so new, and what if the pressure of feeling he has to be where I am right now (pressure I really don't want to put on him) makes him doubt whether this is really what he wants?

So instead I shrug. "Well, I've played a character who was in love with an abusive pimp, soooo . . ."

"That's right! Okay, I guess Tyler's looking pretty good, comparatively." He frowns at the page again. "You know," he says after a moment, "it would be pretty cool to play a really bad character. Like, someone truly awful, but not in some mustache-twirling way. Someone with complexity. Not that I don't love the goofy side-kick role or the guy who gets to be with the hottest woman in the world." He tickles me just to the side of my knee, which is where I am weirdly the most ticklish, and smiles when I giggle. But his expression slides quickly back into serious. "But I think it would be cool to see if I could do it. Is that crazy?"

He looks up at me like he's honestly interested in knowing whether an actor wanting to play a different kind of role is crazy.

But what he's really asking is if I think he can.

"You should absolutely go for a role like that." I start ticking off the reasons with my fingers. "One, you have way better range than you give yourself credit for, and doing those kinds of roles will only expand that range. Two, the more people see you in different types of roles, especially early in your career, the less likely you are to be typecast. And three—" I grin at him. "It's *so* much fun."

He grins back. "Yeah, okay. But. Um. You really think I could do that?"

"I do." I straighten against the headboard, already thinking it through. "You'll want to make sure your agent is scouting for some really good indie roles. They don't generally get as much popular acclaim, but it's a great way to get industry cred, which will open up more doors for you, not to mention the fact that indies—the really good ones—can have some of the most interesting characters. I actually just read a script not long ago that was fantastic. I had to pass on it because the shooting schedule conflicted with another film I'm doing, but there's a role in there you'd be perfect for. I could see if they're still auditioning, and—"

I cut off, realizing he's staring at me, wide-eyed. I grimace. "Sorry. I'm not trying to micro-manage your career, I promise. I get carried away with this kind of stuff sometimes."

"No, that's—that sounds like really good advice. Definitely something to think about." He doesn't look entirely convinced yet, but I get it. It's scary as hell to put yourself out there for something you want badly but aren't sure you're good enough for.

I just hope that over time, he'll realize how very much he is, and not just when it comes to acting. Blake is such a truly incredible person, it's hard for me to believe he wouldn't be good enough for *anything* he wants out of life.

"And," he continues, sitting up so he's right next to me against the headboard, scooting some of the script pages out of the way, "I'm definitely not going to complain that my amazing girlfriend thinks I'm capable of all that."

I smile and shift up under his arm, which is my favorite place to be. Excepting maybe just under *him*. Or on top of him. Or—

I stop myself before I get too far with that train of thought. A train I'm definitely hopping aboard soon, but first . . .

"Speaking of your amazing girlfriend—"

"Which I'm always happy to do."

"We have an important matter to attend to."

"Oh, really," he says in a sly voice that implies this important matter is something that's going to involve us getting naked. Which sounds well worth abandoning all other important matters for, because, damn, THIS MAN.

I can't resist working my fingers up under the hem of his t-shirt, tracing lightly along his abs. "Yes. Our couple name."

His eyelids fluttering closed suddenly becomes a full-on, confused blink. "Our . . . couple name."

"Yep. We're *People* official now. We're an actual couple."

"Good," he says, nodding. "I'm glad *People* finally weighed in and made this possible."

I swat at him. "You know what I mean. Like, in the public eye. But regardless, we need to come up with a couple name for ourselves."

He is trying valiantly to hide his amusement. "Isn't that something other people give you?"

"Sure. If we want to be named something horrid, like 'Blim,' or 'Klake.'" I wrinkle my nose. "The smart celebrities coin their own, but get it spread in a way that doesn't seem like it came from them." I pause. "I mean, I don't actually know that's what anyone does, but it really seems like they should."

"Clearly," he says, in a Very Serious Tone. "I'm guessing you have some ideas?"

"I mean, anything's better than Blim or Klake. So I feel like we've got to use our last names. Like 'Platterson,' or 'Plesserson,' or . . . Oooh, how about 'Watterpless'?" That one actually doesn't sound bad. Kind of catchy.

Now he can't hold it in anymore and laughs. "Isn't that a vegetable?"

"Water*cress* is a vegetable. But I think that's part of what makes it sound catchy. Like, it sounds familiar."

"Awesome. I've always wanted a relationship that reminds

62

people of a vegetable." But he's grinning.

"Really? I mean, I know not *really*, but you think that one's okay? Because if you like it, I can get my publicist on it and get it circulating." I pause, realizing I'm chattering at him a mile a minute again. "Or is this too ridiculous and you're reconsidering your dating choices?"

"Not a chance," he says, shaking his head. Those gorgeous blue-green eyes of his are crinkling adorably at the sides. "This is, however, potentially the most Kim thing ever—which is saying something—and I *love* it. I—" He stops, his cheeks going pink, and looks down at our entwined fingers.

My heart pounds. Was he going to say—

"I, um," he says quietly. "I think I . . . love you."

The warmth and thrill those words send through me—the words I've been too scared to say but longing for, for two weeks now—is immediate and near-overwhelming. My breath is caught in my throat, but I've been wanting to say these words so much that they manage to come out anyway.

"I love you too, Blake."

The expression of stunned wonder on his face is the best way anyone's ever looked at me. "Really?" he asks. He swallows. "Because I should clarify that I don't just think this. I know it. I have for a while now."

I thought I couldn't possibly be happier than I was just seconds ago, but I feel like I'm beaming brighter than a *dozen* floodlights right now. "Yeah, me too."

He's beaming right back at me.

There's this moment of us just grinning at each other like idiots, and suddenly we're kissing madly and shoving script pages off the bed to flutter to the ground. We're pulling off shirts and his shorts and my panties and his boxers. The heat between us is scorching, and we're murmuring how we love each other—finally able to say those words, to hear those words, both of which I somehow feel like I've needed to say to him and hear from him long before we even met, maybe my whole life.

It's desperate and tender, all at once.

It's him and me, all at once.

Which is exactly the way it ends.

We curl up in each other's arms, sweaty and breathing hard, both coming down from those intense highs, the sound of our joined cries of climax still echoing in my mind, along with the sound of what he whispered just before:

I love you, Kim. I love you.

I sigh in utter, contented bliss, listening to his beating heart as he runs his fingers over and over through my hair—which has long since come free of that messy bun.

We just lie there in that dreamy state for a few minutes, and then he says, "By the way, I found your cap."

He reaches down by his legs and pulls out my purple highlighter cap. I squeal excitedly, which makes him laugh.

"If I hadn't just heard you make even happier noises than that, I might be jealous of your markers," he says.

I tilt up to kiss him. "I like the feel of you in my hands way better."

But I quickly snatch the cap from his hands and roll over to snap it on my drying-out highlighter with a very satisfied sigh.

Then I roll back to him and we're both lying on our sides facing each other, arms around waists, fingers stroking along skin.

"What am I going to do when you aren't living, like, ten feet away from me anymore?" he says teasingly.

I don't want to admit how much I've been dreading that, silly though it is. It's not like we don't have cars.

"It's going to be the worst." I trace my nail gently along his side in a way I know he likes. "I've gotten super spoiled with this arrangement."

"Seriously. I live a whole half hour from your house. That's a hell of a lot of driving time that could be spent much more productively."

"Mmmm," I agree. He's told me the neighborhood his apartment's in before, and I might have already looked that distance up, too. "Well," I say, keeping my voice deliberately light. "Maybe you should move closer."

"Yeah?" His voice seems extra light, too, but he's watching me carefully. "Closer would be good."

My heart is fluttering in my chest. Is he actually considering this? Moving, just to be a little closer to me?

That he's even thinking about it is incredible. Though I'm not sure he's thinking quite as close as I'd like him to be.

"You mean, like, get an apartment in your neighborhood?" he asks. "Are there any good ones?"

Yeah, definitely not as close. "There are some that are pretty great," I say lamely, my pulse picking up at what I want to suggest, but know I shouldn't. Should I? "And clearly you need to be living somewhere great."

"Clearly." He sucks his lips inward. "I could probably find someone to take over the rest of my lease. If you think these apartments by you have openings. I mean, if that's what you'd want."

He is considering this. Offering, even.

"Yeah, that would be—I mean, if *you'd* want that, it would be—"

"Pretty great?" He smiles. "Because okay. I could do that." The smile is genuine, but there's something to it that seems a little guarded. A little unsure.

I'm wondering if I should backpedal, make it clear I don't expect anything like that from him—which I don't—but instead I find myself spinning the opposite direction entirely. "Or, you know, if you want to live really close," I say slowly, afraid to meet his eyes, "you could just move in with me."

"Really?"

I look up to see his wide grin, no reservations in it at all. I grin right back at him, my whole body feeling light, but not in some deliberately casual way. Just in a so, so happy way.

"Yeah, really. But be forewarned, living with me means lots of pets with no small amount of suppository needs."

His brow furrows. "So those apartments you mentioned—"

I poke him in the side and he laughs, drawing me closer. "We're moving in together," he says, with that same kind of stunned wonder from when we first said we loved each other.

"We're moving in together," I repeat, feeling pretty full of wonder myself.

He loves me and I love him. We're going to live together. Start a life together.

More than any amount of intricately highlighting scripts, this seems to banish all those worries from my head, to make everything that is difficult survivable and everything that is good possible.

"We're going to celebrate," I say, sitting up and reaching over the bed for my shirt.

"By putting *on* clothes?"

"No. The celebration will definitely be naked. But I feel weird talking to my parents without clothes on. Especially when I'm telling them all about my incredible boyfriend who I'm completely in love with and absolutely moving in with and how it's so awesome that I have parents who love me so much that they can be happy for me about both of these things."

"And if your parents love you so much but *aren't* happy about those things?"

"Then I'll remind them that I'm a big girl who can make her own decisions. And that this is a really damn good one."

He smiles. "I'm not going to argue with that."

I hope they won't either, but even if they do, it's okay. They, like Blake's dad, can be wrong.

I can be a professional, focused actress, and I can also be with a man I met as my co-star, but who I love unreservedly, in a real way that goes so far beyond words on a script.

With Blake, I feel like I can have and be everything. And I hope I can give him even a little of that feeling in return.

SEVEN

Blake
Six and a half Years Before

Kim and I sit in the back of the limo approaching the Chinese Theater, waiting for our turn to walk the red carpet. Kim's wearing this gorgeous blue dress with layers of chiffon that flow off her like waves in the ocean. Her blond hair is pinned up on one side and draping in curls down the other, and she looks like the perfect mix of Old Hollywood glamour and New Hollywood sexy. She's always gorgeous no matter what she wears, but one of the perks of our field is getting to dress up with her like this and show off on the red carpet.

And damn, do we have an audience to show off for. Over the year and a half we've been together, we've amassed a couple-fandom that's both massive and intimidating. When *Over It* released, Kim was already a household name and I was generating buzz, but the spotlight we occupy together has grown brighter and brighter, catapulting the two of us to a level of superstardom neither of us ever imagined. I'm pretty sure it all dates back to Kim's coining of the name "Watterpless," but we are now officially Hollywood's It couple.

Which means that we can both pick and choose our roles,

and we have, doing several more movies together, and increasingly large blockbusters apart. Tonight, though, is the debut of my first indie film, a classic tragedy in which I'm playing a stone-cold hit man. I'm nervous as hell about the reception—it's one thing to be in demand because you're a tabloid darling and another to be perceived as a versatile actor and get offered really challenging roles.

I'm still not sure I'm good enough to compete with all the incredible talent that's out there, but Kim convinced me to ask my agent, Camilla, to find me some indie work, and when this role came along, Kim also convinced me to give it a try.

If my performance is terrible, that's my own fault, but if this turns out to have been a good career move, I owe it all to Kim.

Kim reaches over and squeezes my hand. "You ready for this?"

"The movie? Or the press?"

She laughs, though it sounds strained. The press has been crazy, especially over the last year, as we've featured on every entertainment magazine cover, respectable and tabloid alike. But Kim usually doesn't get nervous for red carpet events, where the press are much less likely to make a scene, as opposed to the random tabloid reporters who now follow us everywhere. We've stopped driving ourselves places and hired private security, which is wild to me.

"The movie," she says. "And the frenzy of press that will be generated by your inevitably amazing performance."

"No pressure," I say, and Kim squeezes tighter. Her confidence in me is exhilarating, but it's also terrifying. I know exactly how lucky I am to have had an incredible year and a half with this woman, and I'm afraid every day that my luck is going to somehow run out.

Kim takes a deep breath and rubs her forehead.

"Are you okay?" I ask.

"Yes," she says. "I've just been feeling a bit off today. I think I might be coming down with something."

"We don't have to stay for the movie. We could have the

driver pick us up around back after we go inside." We've done this before—been seen on the red carpet and then skipped out on the screening. Never for a movie one of us was starring in, but there's a first time for everything.

"No way," Kim says firmly. "This is your night, and I'm not going to miss a minute of it."

Maybe I'm the one who wants to skip out. I don't have a hard time watching myself on screen, but most of my roles haven't felt difficult. I had to work my ass off for this one, and I have no idea if the work paid off.

"Here we go." She fluffs out her skirts then steadies herself on the edge of the seat as the limo rolls up to the end of the red carpet.

"Are you sure—" I say, but then the driver opens the door, and Kim climbs out of the car as gracefully as always. I follow her out and put a hand on her back, and already every camera has turned toward us, flashes blinding us from all sides.

I smile, which feels natural because I'm with Kim. The press may be a pain when I want to do something normal like go surfing or visit my family, but at an event like this, they are definitely on our side, documenting our every move, making our perceived demand skyrocket, which in turn boosts both our salaries and our job opportunities.

We're rocking this career thing, Kim and I, and I hope we're going to be able to do this together for many years to come.

She reaches for me, and I drop my hand from her back to offer her my arm. She clings to it much more tightly than usual, and I wonder if she isn't feeling worse than she let on, if she needs to take something and lie down. I'm not going to ask her here, though. Kim is already pulling me forward, and I walk with her up the carpet, smiling for the cameras. We're nearing the step and repeat, where we'll be expected to turn and smile for dozens—it feels like hundreds—of cameras, and when I look down at Kim, she grimaces slightly before pasting her smile back on.

Okay, something is definitely wrong. I bend down to whisper in her ear. Let the cameras think I'm saying something sexy, but what I really say is, "Do you need to sit?"

She hesitates, then swallows and shakes her head. She doesn't answer, though, just waves me off, and I'm becoming more and more sure that she does and just doesn't want to admit it.

"Kiss her, Blake!" someone yells, which is never something I'm unhappy to do. I turn Kim toward me, putting my finger under her chin and tilting her face up toward mine.

She looks me right in the eyes, and a look of alarm spreads across her gorgeous face.

"Oh, shit," Kim says.

And then she takes a giant step back, doubles over, and vomits right on my shoes.

The cameras are still flashing, but now they're documenting Kim Watterson being sick all over the center of the red carpet, and me standing there staring at her like an idiot with puke all over my Guccis.

"Kim," I say, and I reach for her hand, helping her stand. "Come on." We clearly need to get out of here—no step and repeat for us tonight, though I already know there will be plenty of pictures of this on TMZ within the hour.

She straightens and gives me a look of pure horror. I guide her down the red carpet to the front doors, our security flanking us. I may be tracking vomit as we go, but I'm not going to turn around and find out.

"I need the bathroom," Kim says.

I'm pretty sure we both do. A wide-eyed theater employee takes a good look at my shoes and then escorts us through the lobby and down the stairs to the "ladies lounge." Because security is tight during a red carpet event like this, it's empty, and our security takes up position at the doors while I help Kim into the women's bathroom (thankfully also empty). I hold her hair back while she vomits into a toilet and then stares balefully at the red tile walls of the theater bathroom.

"Oh my god," Kim says. "I just threw up on the red carpet."

I can't help but laugh a little, and Kim even manages a smile as she straightens and lifts the chiffon of her skirt off the gray tile floor.

"Ugh," she says. "Your shoes."

My *shoes.* I kick them off and stuff them under the sink, then grab a paper towel and wet it down to clean off the splash zone of my pant legs. I'm sure this suit is dry clean only. I'm also sure I don't care.

"I thought I'd be okay," she says. "I've been feeling off all day, but I thought if I could just get through our entrance, then we could sit down in the theater, and maybe I wouldn't socialize as much as normal, but everything would be fine." She groans, and I grab her another paper towel to wipe the sweat from her forehead.

"You've got a bug or something," I say. "We'll slip out the back and head home. No one will fault us for it *now.*"

"I don't think it's a bug." Kim says quietly. She steps out of the stall and washes her hands at the sink, then splashes water on her face while I adjust to that statement.

"You don't?"

She chews at her lip. "I'm late."

Oh, shit. "Are you serious?"

She nods at me in the mirror. "Yeah, and remember last month, at Dave Franco's party?"

Oh, *shit.* Kim is usually pretty good about taking her pills, but she missed a few last month and we were using condoms as a backup. Except for the time we both got drunk at Dave Franco's house party and ended up ravaging each other in his coat closet—on a large furry coat that Kim deduced afterward was very likely Rhianna's.

My heart starts pounding and yet skipping beats, all at once. "Oh my god. Are you pregnant?"

She wrings her hands. "I don't know. I was thinking this morning I needed to take a test, but it's your big premiere, and

I didn't want anything to ruin it." She rolls her eyes. "Great job, me."

I step forward and place my hands on her waist. "Stop it. The movie will be the same tomorrow as it is today."

"You should still go," Kim says. "I can get our driver to take me home and come back for you, and then you can still enjoy the night, and maybe when you get back we'll—"

"You're kidding me, right?" I catch her eye in the mirror and shake my head. "I am not going to a premiere to wonder all night if my girlfriend is *pregnant*."

Her face crumples. "Oh my god, what if I am?"

My breath catches. What if she is?

I love Kim more than anything in the world. She's the love of my life, there's no doubt about that. And I want to be with her forever—

But we haven't really talked about the future. Kim is a planner, and I've always figured if she wants more with me, she'll let me know. I absolutely want more with her, but I've never wanted to push her.

"Hey," I say softly. "It'll be okay. We'll figure it out."

She nods, but she's still chewing on her lower lip like she's not at all sure that's the case.

"It must be driving you crazy not to know," I say.

"It is."

"You should have told me you were worrying."

"I know," Kim says. "I just thought we could talk about it tomorrow. Or tonight, after the movie. Probably then, because if I'm pregnant, I'll have to skip the glass of wine."

I smile. It's a tradition we have to come home after a premiere and wind down with a glass of wine. Sometimes we stay in our fancy clothes, and sometimes we change into sweats or nothing at all.

But yeah, if Kim's pregnant—

Oh my god, is it possible we could really have a *child*?

"These are for Ms. Watterson," a female voice says at the

entrance to the lounge, and I step into the doorway and see a theater employee talking to our security. One of our security guards comes over with a water bottle and a fresh towel. I don't know where they got the towel in a movie theater, but we'll take it. Security is blocking the doors to the lounge so I don't think we'll be interrupted. "They say to take your time," our security guard says, then resumes his position at the door.

Take our time. Getting out of here after that display is going to be a zoo. The press is probably going crazy.

My phone rings, and I look at the caller ID. It's my agent, Camilla. She's supposed to be here for the premiere and was going to sit with us during the movie. I answer.

"Hey, Camilla," I say, walking back into the bathroom, grateful I'm getting service down here.

"Is Kim all right? I heard she was sick? I'm sorry I wasn't there. I was planning to meet you inside."

"Kim is okay," I tell her. "They've roped off one of the downstairs bathrooms for us, and I'm a little worried about getting out of the building."

She pauses for a beat, thinking. "When the carpet event is over, we can try to get rid of the press before you leave. It'll be easier if some of them assume you've already snuck off. Do you need medical help?"

"No." I glance over at Kim, who is leaning miserably against the side of a stall. I lower my voice, hoping to keep security from hearing, and, more importantly, anyone beyond. "But we could use a pregnancy test."

Kim's eyes widen, but she doesn't object.

"Blake?" Camilla says. "Did I hear you right? You want me to bring you a—"

"A pregnancy test. Yeah. Though it would probably be good if you didn't announce it."

Oh my god. There have been rumors of a Watterpless baby for the last year and a half. What is the press going to do if there actually is one?

"Okay," Camilla says. "I'll see what I can do. Sit tight."

"We will," I tell her, then hang up the phone.

"Are we really going to take a pregnancy test in the bathroom of the Chinese Theater?" Kim asks.

"Did you want to wait here for an hour for the press to die down and then drive all the way home before you take one?" I ask. "Do we even have one at home?"

"No. If we did, I wouldn't have been able to resist."

I beckon Kim out into the ladies' lounge. The carpet is also red in here and emblazoned with an enormous dragon. The walls are yellow and painted with butterflies, with wall sconces bathing the room in an equally yellow light. There are a couple red leather chairs set off to the side, and we sink down onto them. I scoot mine close enough that Kim can lean her head on my shoulder.

"Are we really going to be okay?" she whispers.

I want to ask her the same. "I'm okay. What about you?"

"I'll be okay with it if you'll be okay with it," she says, and I bend down to kiss her forehead.

"Of course I will." This isn't how I saw this conversation going. Honestly, I assumed that at some point Kim would either decide that she wanted to get married or that she didn't see a future with me, and then we'd either get engaged or break up, though I've seriously tried not to think much about that latter possibility. I've always taken my cues from her—

But I'm realizing now that, if the test is positive, when I ask her to marry me she's going to think it's because of the baby and not because I love her and want to spend the rest of our lives together. Which wouldn't be true at all—I want nothing more than to be with Kim forever, and a baby would just be a convenient excuse to make that official.

God, am I *hoping* she's pregnant?

Either way, I don't want her thinking I'm proposing because I have to.

Can I ask her now? What if she says *no*?

We sit there quietly for a while, and though I know Kim's mind is probably going a mile a minute, I have no idea what she's thinking about all this, and I'm scared as hell to ask.

Footsteps approach, and someone hands a plastic bag to one of our security people, and he brings it back to me. The item inside has been double bagged so it's not clear what it is. I imagine Camilla sent someone down to the convenience store on the corner to have gotten it that fast. She wouldn't want to do it herself, in case someone followed.

"Are you ready for this?" I ask Kim.

"No." She looks ruefully at the bag. "And yes."

"All right then." I help her up. We move back into the bathroom, where she locks herself in a stall.

"Do you need me to hold your skirts?"

Kim groans. "This is ridiculous. But *no*. I will somehow manage to do this without ruining this gorgeous dress or suffering that indignity."

"It's a lot to juggle. Probably a lot like parenthood. Especially all the bodily functions."

"Oh my god, Blake, shut *up*," Kim says, but we're both laughing, and I feel good that, even if this situation is all kinds of awkward, and even if we've unintentionally done something that is going to have a rippling impact on every day for the rest of our lives, at least I can still make her laugh. Kim's always said that's one of the things she loves about me, and while I'm not sure it's all that special, I love that she appreciates it.

"Okay," she says. "I have succeeded in peeing on the stick. And not on my dress—can you imagine if we had to walk out of here with urine on my dress *and* puke on your shoes?"

"Sounds like a party."

Kim emerges from the stall and puts the stick on the counter. "It said to wait two minutes. Can you time it with your phone?"

I set a timer and she drags me back into the ladies' lounge to wait. I don't tell her that I'm pretty sure we'll be able to see the results before that. Kim is an instruction-follower, and this isn't a moment I'm going to argue with her.

I sit down again, but Kim paces back and forth between the yellow lights. Back and forth, back and forth. My phone counts down, but I swear time has slowed. My heart has climbed up somewhere in my throat and is beating like I've run a marathon. I feel like someone has given me a big shove toward a cliff, and I'm about to stumble over the edge and plummet toward the bottom.

It's not because I'm afraid of having a kid with Kim. It's because I know if I don't ask her to spend the rest of her life with me now, I'm going to regret it forever.

"Kim?" My voice breaks, and she looks over at me with terror in her eyes. I know her so well. I know what she's thinking. She's scared I'm going to tell her I can't do this, and I can tell from the look on her face that isn't what she wants to hear.

Instead, I get down on one knee.

Her expression shifts from terror to shock. "What are you—"

"I love you more than anything, Kim," I say. "And I want to be with you forever, regardless of what the test says. I don't want you thinking for the rest of your life that I only asked because you were pregnant."

I'm pretty sure Kim gets where this is going, but I have no idea what she's thinking. My pulse is racing, and I worry that I'm about to have my heart stomped on right here in the bathroom of the Chinese Theater. We're not terribly far from security, so I'm sure they're hearing this. But they've signed NDAs, and if they violate them, well. I don't care.

I have to know.

"Will you marry me?" I ask.

Kim's mouth falls open and her eyes well up with tears. "Yes!" she says. "Yes, yes." She comes over and kneels down beside me and throws her arms around me so hard she almost knocks us both over. I hold her face in my hands and kiss her.

I kiss the woman I'm going to marry.

"Oh my god, that was terrifying," I admit, when we pull

back. "I was so scared you'd say no."

"Of course not," Kim says, smiling at me, her eyes still shining with tears. "I decided a long time ago that if you asked me to marry you, I'd say yes."

"Seriously? How long ago?"

"About two months after we moved in together."

"*That* long ago? You could have *told* me."

She shrugs. "I wanted you to ask when you were ready. I didn't care how long it took."

"I would have been *ready* a long time ago if I knew there was a chance in hell you'd say *yes*."

I blink, letting that sink in. If Kim had said something—any-thing—about this over the last year, she'd already be my wife.

I want that more than anything.

My cell phone beeps. Time's up.

Kim sits back on her heels, and we look at each other. "This is it," she says. "Moment of truth."

"But you'll marry me no matter what," I say. "Right?"

She grins and wipes away a tear with the back of her hand. "Of course I will. No matter what."

I take her hand, helping her to her feet. Then we walk into the bathroom and look down at the two lines.

And I realize I have absolutely no idea what that means.

"Kim?" I say. "You read the instructions, right?"

The tears are streaking down her cheeks now, and she nods. Of course she did. She's Kim. "We're going to have a baby."

While I don't think I was certain until that moment how I was going to feel about that, I grin.

I've never been happier in my life.

EIGHT

Kim

We're having a girl.

We're going to have a *daughter*.

It's surreal and so exciting I can barely contain myself on the ride home from the obstetrician. Blake is feeling the same. I can tell by the looks we keep shooting each other—stunned glances and wide grins and laughs over pretty much nothing at all.

We'd feel the same way if we were having a boy. It's not so much the gender itself as the knowing. Just like when we first heard that heartbeat, it makes it all that much more real. That much closer to meeting our child, who is made from us and yet will be wholly their own person.

It's thrilling and terrifying and thrilling all over again.

"Wow," Blake says for, like, the fifth time.

"Wow," I agree.

We look at each other, both wide-eyed, and we hold hands as we sit in the backseat of the car with LA whizzing by outside. Blake and I still like to drive ourselves when we can, but the constant paparazzi and need for security has made it increasingly difficult to do much of anything by ourselves outside of our own house. It's definitely gotten worse since my little red carpet mishap. The rumors about me being pregnant spread like wildfire, and we didn't see much reason in waiting beyond the first ultrasound to publicly confirm it.

I do think that confirmation helped the overall feeding frenzy of paparazzi desperation, but only by a little. They may not need pics of me leaving the doctor's office to officially prove the rumor true, but it doesn't mean the public doesn't want those pictures anyway. Thankfully, my doctor has a number of celebrity patients and thus also has private entrances and exits. I may be used to having pictures taken of me at everything from movie premieres to walking Chandler Bing, but I like to keep some experiences for just Blake and me, and the space to have this happy/stunned/giddy reaction to finding out the gender of our baby is one of them.

Blake rubs his thumb along the outside of mine. "I love you," he says.

I smile up at him. "Is that for me or our future daughter?"

"Both," he says, bringing my hand up to his lips and kissing the back of it.

There's no better answer in the world than that.

"I love you too," I say back. "Both."

I don't know this little girl yet besides the sound of a heartbeat and some grainy pictures that only vaguely look like a baby, but I know this is so true. I already love her.

And god, how I love Blake. More and more as time passes, as these steps that were always somewhere in the future become the present and even better than I'd ever imagined.

I trace the plain platinum wedding band on his finger, something I find myself doing often these last couple months. Remembering how it felt to stand in that gorgeous gazebo on a hill overlooking the ocean and say our vows. To slip that ring on his hand and have him put a wedding band on mine, the symbols of those very vows, of us promising ourselves to each other forever.

It was the very best day of my entire life.

We kept the wedding small so the press wouldn't be all over it, but it was still so gorgeous. One advantage of celebrity and fortune (of which there are many, despite the drawbacks) is that putting together a wedding in a month and a half that managed to incorporate everything we want was actually doable.

What was less doable was my parents being able to act thrilled about the whole thing, but they did try, at least. Probably by focusing on how legitimately excited they are for a grandchild. It kills me that after all this time, they still don't like Blake. They think he's not right for me, that he's not going to take his responsibilities to me or any future family seriously. They think lots of things about him that are completely asinine and offensive, but they very quickly stopped saying those things when I told them, way back in the first month of Blake and me living together, that if they couldn't keep from belittling him (which they did passive-aggressively in front of him and openly to me when he wasn't around) that they would lose me from their lives.

"You don't have to love him," I said, though to this day, I still can't believe how the people who love me so much couldn't, even if just for how happy he makes me. "But you have to treat him and our relationship with respect."

It was hard to make that ultimatum, but something about it was incredibly freeing. It wasn't until I finally dropped the hammer like this that I realized how under their control I'd been, even as an adult. How much I was suffocated by that.

They love me and they gave up so much of their lives for me. But I don't owe them control over the rest of mine, and I definitely don't owe them the right to hurt the man I love.

It strained my relationship with them for a good, long while, but I think that's getting better. And it's sure as hell a lot healthier.

I wish I could say the same for Blake's relationship with his dad, but really, the guy just avoids us as much as possible and doesn't say much beyond small talk when we're around. It's better than constant criticism, but I know it still hurts Blake. Between my parents and his dad making him feel worse about himself, if it wasn't for Blake's awesome mom and sister, who are nothing but supportive and kind, I would be tempted to disavow extended family entirely.

There have been many times I've been tempted anyway.

We get home, and when we open the door, we are instantly greeted by Ugly Naked Pig, who snuffles around at our feet like he's hoping we've trailed in something edible.

"Hey, little guy," Blake says with a grin. "You're going to have a sister." He scratches Ugly Naked Pig on his head, and the pig backs up to snuffle at Blake's hand. Ugly Naked Pig isn't particularly little, and wasn't even when I first brought him home for Blake as a moving-in-together gift. Blake immediately came up with the most perfect, *Friends*-themed name.

I laugh. "I'm sure she'll be appreciate being known as Ugly Naked Pig's little sister."

"They'll be tight. She'll be raised among the animals, like *The Jungle Book* but with incontinent, three-legged dogs."

"Chandler Bing's not incontinent!"

As if summoned by his name, Chandler Bing hobbles out from the living room, eyes us, and turns back around, like he's not sure why he bothered getting up.

"He's not incontinent *yet*," Blake points out.

He's probably not wrong. Chandler Bing is getting pretty old.

That's a worry for another day. I tug Blake's arm, pulling him to the love seat and flopping us both down on it. "Okay. Time to talk names."

"Not wasting any time, I see," Blake says, not at all surprised and definitely amused.

I turn to the side so my legs are across his lap. "Not that we have to settle on a name today, but—"

"But we should definitely settle on a name today."

He's smiling and I'm smiling, but I feel a little flash of irritation and also embarrassment. I know I can be pushy sometimes in my need to plan, but it's not like I'm totally unreasonable about it.

Am I?

I shove that aside. It's just a joke, no big deal. "No, really. Naming our child is a big decision. It's more important to get it right than to get it done today."

Even as I say that, I feel my nerves start to hum. This really is a huge decision. This is going to be a big part of her identity for her whole life.

What if we mess her up somehow by saddling her with some name she hates? She's already going to have to deal with being the child of Watterpless and all the constant scrutiny that entails.

Blake looks like he might argue with the notion of "getting it right," but he nods instead. "Okay. Names." He pulls out his phone and I do too, both of us Googling baby name lists.

There is one name that has been circling through my mind in this glowy way ever since the car ride home. I don't want to put too much pressure on Blake by telling him that, though.

"What about Abigail?" I say.

He shrugs, looking at the names on his phone. "Eh. Kind of sounds like an old lady name, yeah?"

The disappointment is sharp and immediate. I guess I liked that name even more than I thought, but I try to keep my tone light. "An old lady name? Abby?"

"I mean, more Abigail, but—" He looks up at me and cuts off. "But if you really like that name, then . . ."

"I do, but you don't. So we'll scrap that." I start scanning the names on my phone, but it's hard to pay attention to them while feeling him watch me intently.

"I didn't realize there was anything to scrap," he says after a moment. "I thought it was just a suggestion."

"It was. And one we should scrap." My voice is starting to get a sharp edge to it, which I hate. It was just a suggestion, and maybe not a great one, anyway. I haven't really looked at the other names yet. I'm sure there's a much better one that will be a much better fit.

"Yeah, okay," he says, but he doesn't sound enthused about it. One of his hands strokes along my calf. He looks back at the screen. "How about Sophia?"

I laugh, but that also sounds too sharp. "And that doesn't sound like an old lady name? That's literally the name of one of *The Golden Girls*." Though, admittedly, I do like the name.

He sighs. "Kim, if you like Abigail—"

I frown at him. "Then we'll name our daughter that, even if *you* don't like it?"

"I didn't say I don't like it." His voice is getting testy, too.

"You said 'Eh, it's an old lady name,'" I remind him.

"I said it *kind of* sounds like an old lady name. And even if so, it's not like I'm going to look at our baby and think she's an old lady. It'll be her name, so—"

"Except it's not going to be, because you should love your daughter's name on its own and not just because I picked it." My irritation is growing, but it's not just at him—though there's definitely that—and it's not just irritation. It's guilt and fear.

What kind of wife am I, if I make him feel like he has to pick a name for our child that he doesn't even like, just because I do? I know he lets me have my way a lot, because he's way more chill than I am about most everything. But what if it's not so much that he doesn't have a strong opinion on things, but more about him feeling like he needs to appease me?

Am I really so unreasonable?

Is that the way I'll be as a parent, too? Controlling and smothering them all, even if out of love, just like my parents?

I wet my lips. I can feel my muscles getting tight, my chest feeling like it's sinking inward, giving me less space to breathe. I don't want to be like that. I want him to be able to have equal say in this, for our daughter to have a name he loves and is proud of.

I also want him to *want* that for himself.

"Please," I say, my voice as even as possible. "Let's just drop it and find some others, okay? Some we both like."

"Sure," he says with a short nod. He scrolls through more names, but he doesn't suggest any of them.

Okay, I guess I can start. "Um . . . Harper? Mia?" I keep scrolling. "Sadie? Anna?"

"Those are all nice. Any of those are good." His voice is way too careful, and I glare at him.

"What?" he asks, clearly annoyed.

"Oh my god, Blake." I swing my feet to the floor and sit up straight. "You're just saying they're nice because I suggested them. I need you to have an actual, *real* opinion."

He rubs at his forehead. "I don't—I guess of those, I like Mia best."

"The best of those? Or do you actually *like* it?"

"I like it. It's a good name." He sure doesn't sound like he's overly fond of it right now, but that's probably just because there's this tension now between us, making something that should be fun and exciting into a miserable chore.

I don't want to do that to either of us, but if we stop now, will we just dread getting back to it later? My thoughts are getting knotted up.

There's more, too. A fear that's wiggling through it all, growing stronger and stronger by the minute:

What if he leaves this totally to me and I pick wrong? What if he resents me for not feeling like he has a say in our child's name? What if my name choice makes our child miserable somehow, and there's something about it that makes it so she's teased or mocked by the whole world, something I don't think of until it's too late?

That can be devastating to a kid, and it'll be all my fault.

I can't do this by myself; I'll mess it up if I do.

"Blake—" I start, but then there's a high-pitched yip that makes us both jump.

We both wheel around as Chandler Bing barks again at Janice the Second, the blind Russian Blue cat who mostly avoids everyone, but very occasionally leaps out to give the dog a heart attack. She turns and stalks proudly away, her work done.

I sigh and go to soothe Chandler Bing, but maybe it's that I need some soothing myself.

It's not like Blake and I don't ever fight. We've had fights way worse than this before, about way dumber things. But maybe it's because this feels so important, that this feels so much heavier.

And so much scarier.

I hug Chandler Bing and give him a kiss on his scruffy little head. Then I walk back to the love seat, which suddenly seems so small, like we have to be practically on top of each other. Which normally, I'm all for.

But right now it feels like there's this invisible barrier between us, and throwing myself on his lap while we're both so irritated doesn't seem like the best way to breach it.

Or is it?

"Look," Blake says with a sigh. "How about you make a list of names that you like, and I'll tell you which ones of those I like."

I want to tell him this isn't actually any better than him just picking Mia from among those other names, possibly arbitrarily, but we clearly need some sort of actual plan for this, and official lists are always a good idea.

Also my weakness, which he well knows.

"You'll tell me if you actually like or don't like these names," I say. "Or if you don't like any of them and I should pick more."

He rolls his eyes. "Yes, Kim. I will. And I want you to put the names you love most on it. Even if you think I won't like them." This is pretty pointed, and I know which name in particular he means. Which, fine, I'll put it on, but I still don't know that I can believe him if he suddenly starts gushing about it.

I sit on the cushion next to him—not sprawled across him like before, but our legs are touching. Which does feel better than when they weren't. "Okay, then." I begin scrolling through the names again and making a list on my phone of my favorites. It takes a while, because I want to carefully consider each one, and I expect him to get off the couch and find something more pleasant to do than be in this bubble of frustration, but he doesn't. He just sits here with me, looking through Twitter on his phone.

And him doing that seems to ease the tension—for me, at least—more than a little.

He's still here. He wants to be right here with me, squished up on this love seat, even when we're annoyed with each other and I'm being so . . . *Kim*, and not in the good way.

Finally, my list—which will possibly be the first of several?—is complete. Twelve names that I love, none of which I think will be destructive to our child's future. Especially if Blake honestly weighs in.

"Okay," I say. "Here goes."

I clear my throat and start slowly reading off the names. He does actually appear like he's considering each one, nodding, but waiting until the end of the list to give an opinion. When I reach Abigail, his eyes flick over to me, but he very carefully does the same thing. Consider and nod.

I move on more quickly from that one.

But it's when I reach number ten on the list, "Ivy," that his eyes light up.

"Oh, that's cute," he says.

I smile, much more genuinely than at any other point since we started this. "It is."

He does the same consider and nod face, and I read the last two, neither of which get that reaction.

"So, Ivy, huh?" I ask once we finish.

"I actually like several of the names on that list," he says, and there's something about the way he says it—or maybe the slightly better frame of mind I'm in—that this time I believe him.

"Ivy's the favorite, though." I loved that look on his face when he heard that name.

He gives me a small smile back. "Yeah. I *really* like that one. But honestly, if there's another one you like better—"

"No." I shake my head. "Not for her. Ivy sounds . . . right."

And it does, somehow. Like a puzzle piece locking into place.

"Yeah," he says. "It does."

He tugs my legs back up across his lap, and we look at each

other, and it's back, that excitement for the future, that stunned happiness. Maybe a little muted from the stress of this weird fight, but it's still there.

I haven't ruined anything.

"Ivy," I say, picturing our little baby girl, curled up in our arms.

"Ivy," he says, and puts a gentle hand on my stomach.

We sit there like that for a few quiet, dreaming moments. Then he reaches up and brushes my hair back behind my ear, and says with the most serious of expressions, "The next kid, we're going to use your nineties sitcom system for, right? Because that's a hell of lot easier."

I burst out laughing, and he drops the serious act and grins.

It's a combination of that grin and the relief of getting past that tense hurdle and even the way he says "next kid," like he knows that's in our future, too, but all those worries don't feel quite so heavy anymore.

It's Blake and me. Together, we can handle anything.

NINE

Blake
Five Years Before

I've just finished tucking my almost-one-year-old daughter into her own crib in her own room. This is a new thing we're trying—Ivy just outgrew the portable crib in our room, and it's either teach her to sleep in here or give up on ever having a space to ourselves again and move the mostly unused regular crib into our room. Kim's been worried about Ivy sleeping so far away and asked me fifty thousand times if I think it'll really be okay, but I'm pretty sure lots of kids sleep in their own room. She's just across the hall, so it's not like we won't hear her when she cries, even without the intricate baby-monitor system Kim has rigged through the house.

Ivy fell asleep in my arms as I rocked her, and I bend over her crib, doing the careful dance of trying to shift her into her crib while she's still asleep. If she wakes up, she'll be on to me, and then she'll squawk and climb up on her tip toes and whine for me to pick her up again. She can't speak yet except for two words— "Mama" first, of course, and second "Bing!" for Chandler Bing, Kim's increasingly infirm terrier. I'm hoping I'm going to merit third place in that race, but in reality, I'll probably fall somewhere beneath Ugly Naked Pig, and I won't be able to blame Ivy there.

I lower Ivy's limp body onto the mattress and gently slide my arm out from beneath her, holding my breath. I pull my hands out of the crib, and Ivy sighs, bringing her fingers up to her mouth to suck on them.

But she doesn't wake up, thank god. Ivy is stubborn about many things, and resisting bedtime is definitely one of them. I stare down at my daughter, who is feisty and amazing and who ties with her mother for the thing I love most in the entire world. I wonder if I'm being heartless when I say that I really think it'll be okay if she sleeps with two closed doors between us, but I think we all need it.

Kim most of all. This last year has been hard on her. I underestimated how much mommy guilt can be heaped on by all the books and pamphlets and websites Kim insisted on reading. She had to know everything about how best to take care of a baby—of course she did. Kim always reads the instructions, and despite the common joke about how kids don't come with an instruction manual, it turns out there is no end of instruction in the world for how to raise your baby right.

As far as I have observed, though, no two of those many, varied sources agree with each other. Instead of coming with no instructions, it turns out babies come with a whole library of competing voices. I'm pretty good at tuning them all out, I think, but Kim—

To say it's been stressful for her would be the understatement of the century.

I slip out of Ivy's room and leave the door closed. This is the third night I've managed to put her down in her crib, and the first two nights it lasted less than an hour. If I can get an hour and a half out of this stint, I'll know I'm making progress. I close her door as quietly as I can—I wouldn't have known that the ability to shut a door without making so much as a click would be in my top ten necessary skills for fatherhood, but here we are—and head down the hall to find Kim in the living room.

We're still living in the house Kim owned when we first got together. We've talked a few times about moving since we found out Kim was pregnant. This house is in a gated community, so it's more secure, and it's not like we *need* more space, but it's not even close to what we could afford with both of our careers continuing to do so well. Ivy is already set up with a nice college fund after what *People* paid to break her baby photos.

Neither of us really wants to move out of here, though, until we're ready to buy enough land for Kim to start her animal rescue ranch, and after the year we've had, I don't think either of us is feeling ready to jump into that quite yet.

Chandler Bing trots down the hall by my ankles—rather quickly for a geriatric amputee—and looks over his shoulder at me like, "Are you coming? Don't you know it's food time?" I bend down and scratch him behind the ear and then swing through the kitchen to fill his food bowl, which has recently been emptied by Ugly Naked Pig, who has developed a taste for dog food even though he has a perfectly good dish that we keep stocked with veggies. But I've caught Chandler Bing stealing his carrots, so maybe they just have some kind of turf war I'm not aware of.

"Blake?" Kim calls from the living room.

"Coming," I tell her. I give Chandler Bing one more scratch and join Kim on the wrap-around sofa where she's reclining with her laptop. Her hair is pulled back in a messy bun, and she's wearing a loose blouse over a pair of yoga pants.

"What do you think of this stroller?" Kim tilts her laptop screen so I can see it.

I study the stroller in question. It's got three wheels instead of four, and they're almost as big as bike tires. The stroller itself is a deep blue color that reminds me of the ocean. "It's nice," I say. "I like the blue."

She gives me a look. "Okay, but do you think this one would be better?" She changes the browser tab to a stroller that appears nearly identical in all respects, except this one is orange.

"I don't know," I say. "Did you check the reviews?"

"They're both well reviewed. And they both meet the safety standards from the American Association of Pediatrics, obviously."

I smile. "Obviously."

Kim does not smile, because Kim is not joking.

"I think either of those strollers is probably fine," I say. "Is this for when we take Ivy with us to New York?" We're taking a weekend trip at the end of the month for some interviews, and we decided to bring Ivy with us instead of leaving her here with the nanny. At least, I think this is what we decided. There were several long conversations that went into that decision, and I'm not a hundred percent sure where we landed.

"I don't know that I want to take a stroller to New York," she says, frowning at the computer. So we are still taking Ivy. Good to know. "Do you think that would be secure enough?"

I blink at her. "I mean, we'll have security with us. If they can keep fans from mauling us, they can probably surround a stroller."

"Okay, but maybe it would be better to have Ivy in our arms, where we can shield her more easily from cameras."

"Maybe," I say. "If you don't want to take a stroller to New York, we don't have to. If we decide we need one, we could always get one there."

"But I want a stroller for when I take Ivy out in LA."

"Sounds good." I'm pretty sure there *is* a stroller in the coat closet, but if Kim wants a different one, it's not like we can't afford it. We can afford a freaking army of strollers. If that will convince her to be less worried about taking Ivy out, I'm all for it.

"So which one do you think will be better?" Kim asks.

I motion for her to give me the laptop, and I read over the info for both of the strollers. They're jogging strollers, I learn, and one of them is a BOB, though I'm not sure if that's a brand or an acronym. Possibly it is both.

"Are you thinking of jogging in LA?" I ask.

"No," she says. We both exercise, of course, but we have a home gym with a treadmill and an elliptical. "But I thought it would be nice to have a stroller that rolls easier. Do you think a regular stroller would be better?"

I don't honestly know the difference, besides wheel size and number. Or maybe that is the only difference? "No, I think either one of these would be fine."

Kim gives me an annoyed look. "This stroller is going to be used to transport your daughter. You have to have an opinion."

"This one, then," I say, clicking back to the blue one.

She narrows her eyes. "Are you just saying that because it's blue?"

This is clearly not the correct answer, but it is the truth. "Um, I like the *shade* of blue—"

"Blake!" she snaps. "This is your daughter's safety we're talking about. Can you please base your opinion on something more substantial?"

"You said they were both safety rated. And the reviews are good. I think either one you pick will be fine."

Kim closes her eyes and reclines her head. There are dark circles under her eyes, probably from not getting enough sleep. I've been hoping having Ivy sleep in the other room will help, but so far we haven't actually achieved that. At this rate, Ivy will be four before it happens. "I don't know which one would be better," she says. "I want you to choose."

"Okay. I choose the blue one."

Kim opens her eyes to glare at me.

"Not because it's blue," I say quickly. "But because I think it will be better."

"Why do you think that?"

"Oh my god, Kim," I say, not able to hide my own growing irritation. "I don't know. It's just a stroller. You've read up on this more than I have. If you already know what the right answer is, just tell me and stop making me guess."

"I don't know what it is! That's why I want *you* to form an opinion."

"Do you?" I snap back. "Because it seems like whatever I say is wrong."

"I just think your opinion should be *based* on something."

Ugly Naked Pig wanders into the room and starts nuzzling my leg with his snout. I love that pig, but he lacks the ability to read the room. Chandler Bing isn't much of a therapy animal, but at least he has the sense to run off and hide when Kim and I fight—something that's been happening more and more frequently.

"Do you want me to make the decision or not?" I ask.

We glare at each other for a minute, then Kim sighs. "Yes. But I think you need to do research first."

"I'm not going to write a dissertation about strollers. It's just a stroller." I don't feel like I should have to defend myself here. It's not like they put strollers on the market that are so terrible they won't function, and if they did, it would have bad reviews. Or get quickly recalled, and heaven knows Kim has signed up for notifications of recalls on every piece of baby equipment we own, so we will definitely know about it.

"Fine," Kim says, tearing her laptop away from me. "Don't help, then."

She snaps the laptop closed and glares at it, though I know that's meant for me. I take a deep breath and try to calm down. This fight is stupid. We are fighting about literally nothing. We already *have* a stroller, for god's sake.

But underneath the frustration, there's a pit in my gut. I've been feeling like this a lot lately, so useless, like I can't do anything right. And yeah, Kim is being unreasonable, but I feel like if I were meeting her needs, she wouldn't be frazzled to the point of yelling at me about stupid things that are obviously not the problem.

I need to do better.

"I'm sorry," I say. "We've been doing this a lot lately."

Kim nods and massages her temples. I want to take her hand,

but it would break my heart if she pulled it away. "Do you think there's something wrong with us?" she asks.

That pit grows wider.

"No," I say, because god, if there is, I wouldn't know where to begin fixing it. "We're just tired. Babies are hard, and work has been stressful." We've both worked a little less over the last year, but probably not as much less as we should have. We've had fights about that, too, where Kim asks me if I think it's okay if she does this event or says yes to this role, and I tell her it's fine and she argues that maybe it won't be fine, and I can't know if it will, because I didn't really take the time to think about it.

She's probably right. I don't think about things as deeply as she does, and now that I have a kid, I probably should.

"Maybe things would be easier," she says quietly, "if we weren't always getting in each other's way."

Everything goes still.

"What do you mean?" I ask.

She gives a tiny shrug, and I'm pretty sure I get what she means. If I weren't here to fight with, she probably would have bought the damn stroller and not thought twice about it. The problem isn't a stroller, or how often she gets out of the house, or even which room Ivy sleeps in. The problem is us.

And when she says she thinks things would be easier for us, she means they would be easier for *her*.

"I don't know," I say around the lump making my throat tight, trying to keep my voice even. Light. "I wouldn't want to be the only one getting up at night. Would you?"

Kim's still not meeting my eyes, her hands clutching the laptop tightly. "Is that the only reason we're still together?" she asks, even more quietly than before.

Oh my god. *Is* it? Things are hard, yeah, but Kim is still my rock. I love her more now than I did when we got married, something I couldn't have imagined was possible then.

But I've always known how lucky I am to be with Kim. I've always known maybe someday that luck was going to run out.

"It isn't for me," I say. "I'm still in this."

"Really?" Her blue eyes are teary.

"Yeah, really." I'm not sure how *that* could even be a question. "Even if I suck at picking out strollers."

One corner of Kim's mouth turns up, and relief floods through me. If she's smiling, she's not leaving me. Everything else we can work through.

I wish I could make her laugh right now, but I'm afraid to try. God knows I'd probably say the wrong thing. I don't ever seem to be able to make her laugh like I used to.

"I love you," I say.

"I love you, too," she says.

My eyes close as I soak in those words. Things are difficult, but she still loves me.

I find myself wondering, though, how much longer that's going to last.

TEN

Kim
Hours Before

I'm sitting on a stool at the kitchen counter, staring down at our little baby boy, who is sleeping soundly in his bouncy chair. Lukas, who is six months old now, is a much better sleeper than Ivy ever was. Or still is, because Ivy's six now and I'm not sure that girl's ever gotten a full eight hours of sleep. Fortunately, it's been a long while since she's needed to wake us up to join her, and she just plays in her room until one of us rolls out of bed.

I should be happy that Luke can sleep so soundly and for long stretches. I should be happy, but I'm increasingly not. The worries are getting worse and worse, spinning through my brain nearly constantly.

Maybe he's sleeping too much. Maybe he's sleeping too soundly. I can't stop checking on him during the night, afraid of SIDS, afraid my baby won't wake up. Hearing his soft breath through the monitor—or even when I'm standing in his room—isn't enough, because maybe I'm just imagining it? Hearing what I desperately want to hear?

The only way I can feel better is by putting my hand on his

chest, feeling the gentle rise and fall. The little heartbeat beneath my fingers. I'll breathe a sigh of relief, because that finally quiets the fears.

Except there are some nights—okay, many nights—when I crawl back into bed and try to go to sleep, but I can't, because suddenly I'm afraid I didn't check him right. Or maybe I'm just remembering how I checked him last night, and I didn't actually do it tonight at all. Having a baby is stressful and I'm sleep-deprived, as Blake often reminds me. And maybe, even if I did check, Luke has stopped breathing since then. It could happen at any moment, couldn't it?

Better to be safe than sorry, I always think, climbing out of bed again. It's our child's life at stake.

I'm checking and checking, waiting and watching, and every time, he's breathing. But I still live in fear that maybe next time I'll find that he's not.

I know these thoughts aren't rational. I know it, but I can't stop. Never for long.

Now I stare at Luke, with his eyes fluttering in sleep and his small hands clutching the edge of his fuzzy blanket, and my heart is so full, bursting with love.

What if I were to lose him? What if I were to lose any of them?

A hard knot forms in my chest, as it does more often than not. Because losing Blake—not in death, thank god, but from my life—is a shadow that hangs over me every minute.

As if that thought summons him, he walks into the kitchen, headed to the fridge. He sees me and falters a step. "Hey," he says. Softly. Too casually. God, he has to act too casual around me, step so carefully. This is what we've become.

This is what I'm doing to us.

"Hey," I say back. I drum my fingers on the granite counter-top, but stop immediately, afraid to wake Lukas.

Blake continues to the fridge, opening it and taking out a Gatorade—blue, his favorite. He's sweaty from a workout, his auburn hair sticking to his head, his shirt clinging to him. He's gorgeous as ever. Somehow more so as the years go on. "I, um. I thought you'd gone to your parents' already," he says.

"Luke fell asleep while I was giving Carlton his calcium drops, and I didn't want to wake him up to get him in the car." We have several more pets now, besides Janice the Second and Ugly Naked Pig. Chandler Bing passed away, but we've got another two dogs, one with liver problems and one who had been abused, and a bearded dragon (the aforementioned Carlton) with metabolic bone disease. We did run out of *Friends* names, so we've moved on to *Fresh Prince of Bel-Air*.

It's a far cry from the number of animals I hope we'll be able to help when we can start our ranch, but we're still helping some of them.

I wish I could do more, do better. For the animals. For my children. For Blake. For our marriage. But when it comes to that, it's like I'm running on a treadmill that's too fast for me to keep up, only moving me farther and farther backward.

"Makes sense," he says. He takes a long drink of the Gatorade.

I look back at Luke. Our little baby, sleeping soundly. Too heavily? The words scratch at my brain. Babies are supposed to sleep flat on their backs, not in bouncy chairs. Have I left him too long? Am I a bad mother, because I'm afraid to move him, selfishly soaking up these few minutes of sleep, all the while putting his life in danger?

He's breathing, though. There's even a spot of pink in his cheeks.

Pinker than before? Close to a feverish red, even?

My throat goes dry. I shouldn't ask. I shouldn't.

But I do anyway, because I need to know.

"Do you think he's too warm?"

Blake slowly sets down his drink, and I can see the instant wariness in his eyes. Those eyes that used to shine with joy when they'd look at me, crinkling at the sides with his smile. When was the last time I saw him look at me that way? When was the last time I saw that sunshine smile, undimmed with this wariness, this unhappiness? I see it when he's playing horses with Ivy or making Luke giggle.

But when was the last time I saw it for me?

His gaze flicks down to Luke for the barest second. "Probably not."

"You didn't even look," I say, frustrated. Shit, it's happening again, I can already tell. Another fight.

But can't he just *really* look? Can't he just take a minute and check, so I don't always have to? Just to quiet my mind, even a little?

I get off the stool and kneel by Luke, pressing my fingers to his forehead. It does feel warm, but I was a bit cold in here, which is why I put the blanket on him in the first place. Also, it's his favorite blanket, and he seems to sleep even better with it, and if he sleeps so much, that probably means he needs it, right? But babies aren't supposed to sleep with blankets, because they could cover their faces, so I never do that when I put him down in his crib, which I'm always supposed to do when he sleeps. But I didn't, not this time, and maybe I should.

Blake steps closer, looking down at Luke, and I can tell that my husband is barely holding in an equally frustrated snap back, his jaw clenched tight around it. "He looks fine, Kim," he says.

"Does he? Those red spots on his cheeks—"

"Then take the blanket off him." Tossed off so quickly, even though he can't possibly have thought through if that's the best thing to do.

I glare at him. My fear is spiking, which lately seems to always bring anger with it, too. What if I make the wrong choice? Why can't he *help* me, so I don't? "Do you *actually* think I should? Or are you just saying that so you don't have to deal with me? Because it doesn't seem too much to expect you to give this some real thought—"

He throws his hands up in the air. "Oh my god, Kim, are we doing this again?"

I sit back, squeezing my eyes shut. We *are* doing this again. Or maybe we just never stop.

Maybe I can't ever stop.

It feels like it's always been this way, but I know it hasn't. We had a really rough patch for a while after Ivy was born, but we got through it. It got better, so much better. We were happy again.

Weren't we?

Yes, we were happy. Our little family of three. Ivy getting bigger and bigger, going from baby to toddler to kindergarten. Faster than either of us were ready for, our little girl growing up. And yeah, there were still fights, and I've always been a worrier, my fears sometimes spinning and spinning, getting the better of me.

But not nearly so often, and the in-between was so good. Blake and I filmed several more movies together—the public can't get enough of Watterpless on-screen—and had a blast doing so. I (mostly) loved my career before I ever met him, but the times I get to film with him are like magic. He makes it fun in ways it never was without him.

Busy as we were, we even took a road trip, just Blake and me. We'd done a big road trip before, but that was back before we had kids. This time felt even more special, getting that time alone for just us. We stopped in little towns and out of the way diners. We spent nearly a full week at a big animal sanctuary in Utah that I'd always wanted to visit, to get a real sense of the kind of ranch I want someday. Doing that with Blake— planning our ranch as we'd lie curled up in each other's arms in roadside motels, laughing and loving and being just *us*, not Watterpless, Hollywood's Favorite Couple . . .

That was magic, too.

We've had *so much* of that over the years. And even after how rough a time we had for a year or so after Ivy was born, we were so, so happy when we found out I was pregnant with Luke. Our beautiful, perfect family somehow becoming even more perfect.

And it did.

But things have gotten bad between Blake and me again these last few months. Not just bad; worse than before. I have everything in the world, and I can't stop being terrified I'll lose it all. I have everything that should make me happier than I've ever been, and I can't stop being miserable.

I'm making him miserable, too. This man who I still love with everything in me—I can see him becoming more and more distant and weary of it all. I can see us, our marriage, being whittled down so thin we're right on the edge of breaking.

Always. And I can't stop it.

I'm becoming less and less sure I should try.

Blake scrubs a hand through his sweat-damp hair. "What do you want me to say, Kim? Because nothing I say is ever enough. You want my opinion, and it's *never* right. So why *the hell* do you keep asking?"

I clench my trembling fists. "I want you to try, Blake. I want you to take me seriously and try—"

"You don't think I take you seriously?" Hurt and anger blaze from those blue-green eyes of his, like a storm over the sea.

I hate that I said that. I hate that right now, it feels true. "You dismiss everything I'm worried about like it's nothing, like I'm worried about *nothing*—"

"Because it *is* nothing! It's a fucking blanket, Kim!"

I jump to my feet. "It's your fucking *son!*"

There's a beat where we stare at each other wide-eyed, like we've both been slapped. We've yelled at each other plenty before, but not like this.

Luke squirms but doesn't wake up. Then there's a sound from the hallway, right around the corner from the kitchen, and, as one, we both look over, and I know we're thinking the same thing. Oh my god, is that Ivy? Did our daughter just hear us swear at each other like that?

Blake steps toward the hallway, but Ugly Naked Pig shuffles by. I feel my heart start again. Limply, like it's thumping just barely enough to keep me alive. Blake is relieved too, I can tell, but he still looks down the hallway anyway, then turns back to the kitchen, shaking his head.

He doesn't look at me, though.

I grip the edge of the counter. Ivy may not have heard us this time—she's upstairs watching a movie, which maybe I should stop anyway, maybe she's had too much screen time today?—but I know she's heard us fight before, way too often.

It isn't just us being hurt. It's our children, too.

I try to force myself to breathe evenly, but I can't. I look back at Luke; his cheeks are still pink, but maybe he really is fine? Maybe he's fine when he's sleeping in his crib at night, even if I forget to check. Maybe Ivy can watch a movie twice in a row and it won't hurt her. Maybe I didn't need to have her hair cut last month, maybe it wouldn't have wrapped around her neck while she slept and—

Maybe Blake's right to dismiss me. Maybe I'm just losing my mind.

Or maybe *I'm* right, and if I don't worry like this, our children are going to die.

I don't know anymore. I feel like I know and then I don't and I'm going to mess it all up, and I just want him to tell me what to do sometimes so that I don't make some terrible mistake. *Please, Blake, just tell me what to do, take this seriously and tell me what to do, I'm going to fall apart, everything's going to fall apart . . .*

"I think there may be something wrong with me," I say softly.

Blake's expression falls even further than before. God, he looks so defeated. He always looks so defeated. "There's nothing wrong with you. You're fine. We're both just stressed, that's all."

It's not the first time I've said that to him, and that's always his answer. Would it still be, if he could see into my mind? If I told him how deep the fears go? If I told him that I can't look at strollers without thinking they're going to fold up and kill my babies? That I can't let Ivy get close to the kitchen sink because all I can picture is the garbage disposal malfunctioning and turning on right when she's reaching in . . .

Blake lets out a sigh, which falls heavily into the silence between us. "Maybe we should look into hiring another nanny," he says. "Take some of the pressure off you."

Off me. Because I'm the one who can't handle this. But I'm also fine. There's nothing wrong with me, except I'm the one who's failing us, tearing us apart. That's what he thinks, and he's probably right.

I don't know that hiring another nanny is the solution, though. Our last nanny, Claire, left a couple months ago to go back to school full time. She was great with the kids, but the truth was, even having a nanny didn't take the pressure off. If anything, it made it worse. Because if she was watching my kids, that meant I wasn't there, and if something went wrong that I could have prevented . . .

"I don't want another nanny," I say firmly. Maybe too firmly. I try to soften it with the next bit. "Not yet, anyway."

Blake nods, still not looking at me. "Okay. Then at least leave Luke with me today. That way you can have some time with your parents without having to worry."

My pulse pounds in my ears. Not having to worry. Except I will.

Normally, this would be a good solution. Unlike with nannies, I don't usually have a problem leaving the kids with Blake. He's their father, after all, and he loves them every bit as much as I do. And even if he doesn't take the time to do the research and the worrying that I do, things that make me so angry when I'm around, I'm not generally afraid of anything bad happening to them under his care.

Because I trust him to keep them safe. It's me I don't trust.

But right now, maybe because I'm the one who noticed Luke's cheeks, who knows of the possibility of him running a fever—

Right now, I *know* that if I don't keep looking back at Luke every few seconds, he's going to die and it'll be all my fault. Not

Blake's, but mine. Because I was the one who knew it would happen, which means I was the one who let it happen.

"No," I say quickly. "I'll take him with. I have to—I'll take him with."

Blake stares at me, like he can't believe this. "You don't trust me with him."

I cringe. "It's not that."

"Right. Sure." The words are clipped. Frustrated.

I don't know how to explain what it is, not without losing him entirely. I know I'm pushing him to the brink. I've already pushed him there, maybe a long time ago.

I've always been neurotic, a worrier. The girl who color-codes her scripts to within an inch of their life because if she doesn't, the whole movie will fall apart. The girl who panics over a dried-out marker and boxes her life into rules so *she* doesn't fall apart. Maybe he's right that there is nothing wrong with me; maybe it's all just who I am. But more and more (and more), I'm realizing that some of the things Blake used to love about me—my strong sense of responsibility for everything around me, this once quirky-seeming need to chart things and make lists and fret about all the details—are things that now make him miserable.

That he's become trapped with me, trapped by our marriage, our life together.

That no matter how desperately I love him and need him, I'm not the right person for him. I'm not the woman who can give him the life and marriage he deserves, the one who will make him truly happy. I'm not the woman he needs or maybe even loves anymore.

I've always been too terrified to ask him outright if he still wants this, to give him the out. Too terrified to know for sure how much he wants to take it. I've teased around the edges of it, telling him things might be easier if he wasn't with me, because I think it would be. Easier for him, definitely, to not have to put up with all of this.

Maybe even easier for me, to not have to see in real time how being with me is chipping away at his happiness, at his light, until all there is when he's with me is . . . this.

He never says outright that it would be easier. He never says outright that it wouldn't.

I need to know. I can't handle knowing.

I really can't breathe now. I can't move, but I have to. I have to go or I'll say these things and it'll be over. I have to go or I won't get the courage to say these things and we'll be stuck in this cycle forever. Both seem equally true.

So with Blake staring forlornly out the window at nothing, I unbuckle Luke from his bouncy chair and scoop him in my arms. He wakes and fusses and I'm failing him too, but I can't be here right now, I can't.

I want to run to Blake, want him to hold me in his arms, want every pain and hurt to vanish.

But even if it would somehow work for me, it wouldn't for him. Not after all this.

I walk out the door and don't look back at him, so he won't see the tears streaming down my face.

ELEVEN

Blake

I'm worried Kim isn't going to come back from her parents' house, but she does later that night, after I've got Ivy in bed. I also worried Ivy was going to ask where her mom went and then I'd have to either lie to her or explain why Kim took Luke to see his grandparents and left Ivy with me, but she didn't even bring it up, probably because she's used to one or the other of us being gone for work. I read her a bedtime story and tucked her in and then cleaned up the kitchen, mostly because I felt terrible about how that whole conversation went, and I want to do something to make Kim's life better.

Especially when all I do lately is make it worse.

Like I always do, I go over and over the conversation in my mind. I can think of a lot of things I should have done better. I should have been more patient. I shouldn't have snapped at her. But it never seems to make it better in practice. No matter how many times I tell myself that next time I'm going to be more understanding and we're going to have a productive conversation and things are going to go better, as soon as we get into it, I feel like I'm sucked right back down in the same problems again. The same pattern, over and over again, fights I can have with myself.

I don't understand why we do it, but it always seems to come down to Kim needing something from me that I don't know how to give her. Something I may never be able to give her.

Something I'm increasingly sure that she doesn't know how to live without.

Kim comes in the door with Luke still in his car seat, but unbuckles him right away like she always does, even though he's asleep. I join her in the entryway with a dishtowel in my hand. "Want me to put him down?" I whisper.

Kim shakes her head. She's already scooping him out of the car seat and onto her shoulder with a fervent "shhhhh."

She doesn't look at me as she passes me, heading to his room.

I take a deep breath. Obviously I need to apologize, but while the sleeping child is being transported is not my moment. I put away the dishtowel and move into the living room, waiting for Kim to come back.

It takes her a long time.

Something feels different this time. Kim doesn't seem angry, more sad and resigned. In the six months since Luke was born, things have been going steadily downhill, worse than when Ivy was a baby. It's only natural, I suppose, that Kim feels my failures as a husband most acutely when there's so many more things to take care of, so many more ways for me to fail her. Having a baby is stressful for everyone, and that stress widens all the cracks in our marriage, all my faults that, at other times, Kim is wonderful enough to ignore.

Until she can't, because she's drowning, and no matter how far I reach, I can't ever seem to pull her from the water.

Kim comes and stands in the doorway and finally makes eye contact with me. Stress and sadness and pain radiates from her, and all I want to do is take that away, but she feels so far away.

I can't even remember the last time I made her laugh.

"I'm sorry," I tell her, and she closes her eyes.

"No, I'm sorry."

I'm not sure there's much for her to be sorry about. She doesn't trust me with Luke, and how can she, when she can hardly trust me with herself?

I wish I knew how to bridge this gap, but I don't. I can't. I've failed to do it so many times, often thinking I'm making progress, only for the cycle to start all over again.

I don't know how to make Kim happy, and it's becoming abundantly clear that I never will.

"How's Luke?" I ask, because I am, first and foremost, a coward, always afraid to face our problems head-on, hoping they'll evaporate if I just ignore them long enough. In my own defense, occasionally they do. But more and more lately, they don't. I'm driving my wife crazy and hurting my family, and I know saying "I'm sorry" doesn't begin to scratch the surface of the pain I've caused Kim by letting her down.

"He's fine," Kim says, and she hugs her arms around herself. I want to get up and put my arms around her and tell her it's all going to be okay, but what right do I have to say that when I'm increasingly sure that it isn't?

She takes a deep breath, like she's steadying herself for something, and then she looks up at me. There's a dead look in her eyes, like she's made a decision, and there will be no going back. "Do you want a divorce?"

The room tunnels around me, until all I can see is Kim, tired and worn down, staring at me from the end of a very thin tube. She's just across the room, but she seems like she's a million miles away.

Do I want a divorce?

I want everything to have gone differently. I want Kim to be happy, first and foremost, and being with me is slowly driving her mad. She's been telling me for years that her life would be easier without me in it. She's talked around the idea of divorce before, hints and implications, but she's never asked me about it outright.

Do I want a divorce?

I want Kim and me to be happy together. I want to start again from the beginning and be better for her, be what she needs.

But I have to live in this reality, with this set of failings and mistakes.

Do I want a divorce?

God, no, I don't. But above all, I don't want to make Kim miserable anymore. This is my chance not to fail her, not to trap her here in a misplaced sense of duty, keeping her prisoner when she wants to be free.

Free to find someone who can give her what she needs. Free to find someone to make her happy the way that she deserves.

Someone not me.

"Yes," I say, and Kim bursts into tears. I wish I could join her, but I haven't shed a single tear since I was a kid, and now it's this wall I can't break through, penning me in. The tunnel is collapsing now, crushing me, everything I wanted for my life imploding. I lost Kim a long time ago, but this final moment is still too terrible for words.

The moment I'm finally doing the right thing and letting her go, even if it kills me.

Kim's shoulders shake as she sobs, but I can't comfort her, not anymore. I've never been good at it, probably because I was always the problem to begin with.

And all I can think is that if I can't make her laugh anymore, the very least I can do is stop making her cry.

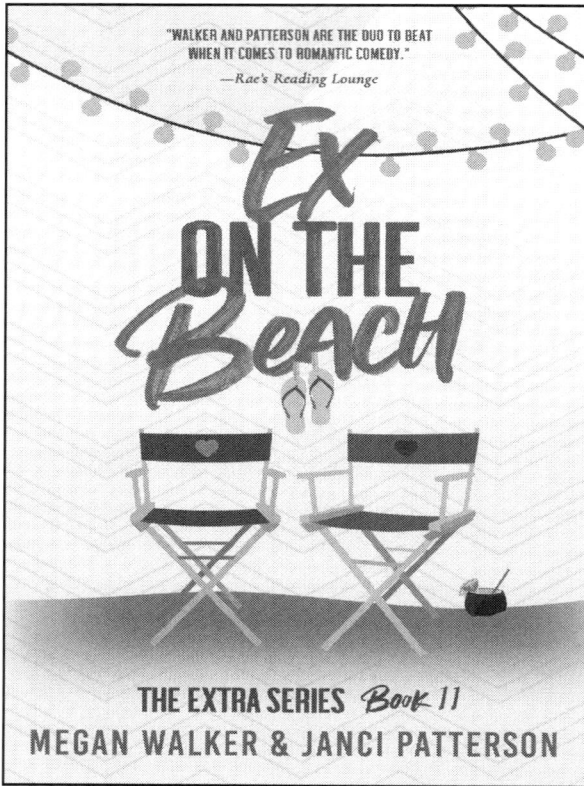

"WALKER AND PATTERSON ARE THE DUO TO BEAT WHEN IT COMES TO ROMANTIC COMEDY."
—*Rae's Reading Lounge*

Ex ON THE Beach

THE EXTRA SERIES *Book 11*

MEGAN WALKER & JANCI PATTERSON

Kim and Blake's story doesn't end there! Read on for the beginning of *Ex on the Beach*, their second chance to find their happily ever after.

ONE

Kim

I've got a plan for this.

Okay, that's not entirely true, given that I don't know the reason my agent needs to meet with me "today, if possible," but telling myself that helps loosen the tension in my chest a bit. I've been with my agent, Josh Rios, for long enough to tell by the tone of his voice that the news isn't great. Probably the Sofia Coppola project next year is getting pushed back—that kind of thing is common, but Josh knows how much I hate my schedule getting messed up. Not just because I've got a stronger emotional attachment to my intricate, color-coded calendar system than most of LA feels for their favorite Botox provider, but because The Schedule is in careful balance with my ex-husband as we manage our time with our kids in between both of our busy film careers.

Messing with The Schedule often means a domino effect of epic proportion, which requires me to actually converse—even if only via text—with Blake.

I pace in the entryway of my house, my sandals clicking against the tile floor. One of my cats, a Maine Coon named Roz, has her huge girth balanced precariously on the stair banister, watching me with her single eye. I pet her on the one spot on her back where she likes to be touched and think through what my plan could be if the Coppola project gets stalled.

I may have to cancel the trip to Australia for the World Surf Championship—which was supposed to be a surprise for my daughter, Ivy. While I'm not particularly sad to miss out on days of watching a sport I don't have any interest in, I was looking forward to seeing her enjoy it. Sharing the part of her life that she normally only shares with her father. Blake is the fun parent. I've long since resigned myself to that fact—I'm the parent that counts the number of vegetables they've eaten and charts their screen time.

I was really excited to be the fun parent, for once.

Not that the kids don't enjoy their time here on the ranch. I know they do. Lots of animals and outdoor space—I have that going for me. And Ivy will be just as excited when the championship comes around in another year, so I could still—

The gate comm buzzes; I glance at the camera and see Josh's sleek Porsche, and I press the button to open the gate. While I wait for him to make his way down the drive and park, I breathe in and out slowly.

Whatever the news is, whatever changes to The Schedule and family plans it entails, I can handle it. No doubt I've handled far worse. Or survived, at least—even if it felt like just barely.

There's a knock, and several dogs begin barking and howling from behind the closed door to the bedroom areas. Their barking sets off more from the dogs outside. It's a familiar chain reaction that never fails to make Luke giggle. He calls it the "Twilight Bark," like from *101 Dalmatians*.

I miss my kids, even though they're just at school right now. No matter how many animals and ranch workers are here at any given time, the house feels a little empty without them. It's worse when they're at their dad's, which they generally are about half the week, unless one or the other of us is off filming on location.

I open the door. Josh Rios is standing there in a nice, fitted suit, his dark hair styled back, looking, as always, every inch the professional. We used to have our business meetings at a restaurant, but the paparazzi are ruthless, attempting to lip-read video footage or sneak in long-range mics to get the scoop on my future projects—or to suggest that my agent and I are having a torrid lunchtime affair over Cobb salads at Angelo's. Now I usually meet him at his office.

His offer to drive all the way out here might mean that the news is worse than a shift in schedule.

He greets me with a handshake and a smile that looks a little tense. Roz greets Josh with a hiss, her back arched, and her lone ear—on the same side of her head as her lone eye—flattened against her head.

"Don't worry about her," I assure Josh, who shoots a wary look at the large ball of angry cat. "She's all talk."

Josh laughs. "I deal with that type a lot." Still, he gives Roz a wide berth as he steps into the sitting room. I feel better about my decision to keep the dogs out of this part of the house. Josh has been to the ranch a couple times over the years, and overall seems to deal well with the animals, but I doubt he'd appreciate the enthusiasm of the roaming pack of house dogs—especially our new short-haired Chihuahua, Urkel, who gleefully humps every pair of men's dress shoes he encounters.

I'm working on getting him to stop, and while I'm not unused to training challenges—most of the animals at my sanctuary here have special medical needs or training problems that make them difficult to place in normal homes—his passion for Italian leather Oxfords might be one of the epic love stories of our time.

"Can I get you anything?" I ask as Josh settles in on the sofa, taking in the view of the ranch from the big picture windows. This room is probably my favorite in the house—the vaulted, exposed timber ceilings and the way the sun streams through the windows, warming the tile. But the best part is definitely the view of the land, dappled with fruit trees and yew pine, with the sunlight sparkling off the duck pond in the distance.

In addition to the land itself, the view also includes numerous buildings I've added—stables, supply huts, chicken coops, medical stations, that sort of thing. One of my ranch workers is driving by on a golf cart loaded with bags of dog food while being chased by about a dozen dogs. There are goats climbing over my patio furniture, chewing on the already ragged edges of my rattan chairs.

I'm usually out there with the animals myself when I can be. Administering meds, training, playing with them. This sanctuary is still my dream come true.

Even if it somehow feels a bit hollow.

Josh starts pulling paperwork out of his briefcase. I'm dying to leap into the reason he's here and get to figuring out a solution, but there's this small-but-persistent part of me that hopes the problem will disappear if I front-load it with enough small talk and caffeine. "Some coffee? Something to eat?"

"No, thanks," he says. "I actually just had a brunch date with Anna-Marie." He smiles when he says his wife's name, like he always does—that reflexive smile of a man deeply in love. I wonder if Blake ever did that when he thought about me, even in the early days.

"Nice," I say, shaking off the thought. It doesn't matter anymore; it hasn't mattered for six years. "Celebrating anything?"

"Just an hour in which our schedules line up. We've learned to steal every chance we get."

I remember how that used to be. Between film schedules and kids' schedules and industry events, some of the best alone time Blake and I had were those midnights we'd order from that all-night Thai place not far from our old house and sit out on the backyard patio under the stars. We'd eat, and talk, and laugh, and toss rice noodles to our pet pig, who'd be snuffling around by our feet.

Sometimes those nights feel so long ago, so out of reach, that it feels like I imagined them entirely.

I sit on the chair across from Josh. "We've still got to arrange a time for you to bring Anna-Marie and your little girl here to see the ranch—what is she now, two? Three? My kids would love to show her around."

Josh's grin widens. I've met Anna-Marie a few times at agency functions, but I've only seen pictures of their gorgeous, dark-haired daughter. Josh Rios can be a shark when it comes to contracts and protecting his clients, but he has an equal reputation for being an unabashed family man—his wife and daughter are the top priorities in his life, and he makes no excuses for that. It's one of the reasons I signed with him. It's rare to find someone in this industry who gets what's really important.

"Riony's two," he says. "And they would love that. Ri's been obsessed with horses lately. Dragons, too, but I'm guessing you have fewer of those."

"Horses we have. I'll work on the dragons." I smile, then let out a breath. We've done enough small talk to make me feel socially competent, and I know the problem—whatever it is—is still waiting for me. "So, what's the bad news?"

Josh nods and sits forward, slipping right into business mode. "In the grand tradition of most things in life, there's both good news and bad news. The good news is that the new Hemlock movie's been green-lighted, and they definitely want you back. They're willing to pay very, very well for this one."

My eyes widen in surprise—this is about Hemlock? After my last two movies playing the comic book character exceeded box office expectations, it was pretty much guaranteed they'd make a third. Playing Hemlock hasn't exactly been the artistic pinnacle of my career, but it's been fun, and I've already told Josh I'd be up for another movie. I can't imagine how this would lead to bad news.

"Okay," I say slowly. "So, what, are we going to be filming in Siberia or something?"

"Close. Miami. In July and August." He pauses. "This July."

My brow furrows. "But that's—"

"Only two months away, yeah. Apparently all the secrecy around this project, all that stuff *I* couldn't even get them to breathe a word on—well, what they've been working on came together all at once, and they want this done fast."

Miami in July sounds a little miserable, but I can handle it. I technically don't have any projects for the next six months. We can tinker with The Schedule to give me more time with the kids before that. Maybe I'll take most of June and—

"That's not the important part," Josh says, his expression reluctant. "This project is a crossover with a romantic subplot. They want Hemlock with Farpoint."

I make a choked sound I'm not particularly proud of, then clear my throat. Farpoint is a character with a rival comics company. He's had several successful box-office hits of his own, all of them starring my ex-husband.

"Farpoint," I say numbly. "So that means . . ."

Josh nods. "That means you'll be starring with Blake."

Keep reading! Grab a copy of Ex on the Beach today.

Other Books in the Extra Series

The Extra
The Girlfriend Stage
Everything We Are
The Jenna Rollins Real Love Tour
Starving with the Stars
My Faire Lady
You are the Story
How Not to Date a Rock Star
Beauty and the Bassist
Su-Lin's Super-Awesome Casual Dating Plan
Ex on the Beach
The Real Not-Wives of Red Rock Canyon
Chasing Prince Charming

Printed in Great Britain
by Amazon